DAYS AND NIGHTS OF LOVE AND WAR

DAYS AND NIGHTS OF LOVE AND WAR

EDUARDO GALEANO

translated by
Judith Brister

foreword by
Sandra Cisneros

"IN DEFENSE OF THE WORD"
Translated by Bobbye S. Ortiz

AAKAR

Days and Nights of Love and War
Eduardo Galeano

First Published in India, 2009
Reprinted 2017
Reprinted 2022

ISBN 978-81-89833-70-1

Published in agreement with Monthly Review Press, New York for publication and sale only in the South Asia

Published by
AAKAR BOOKS
28 E Pocket IV, Mayur Vihar Phase I
Delhi 110 091, India
www.aakarbooks.com

Printed at
D.K. Fine Art Press, Delhi

Everything related here actually happened.
The author has written it down just as his memory retained it. Some names—a few—have been changed.

This book is dedicated to Helena Villagra.

also by EDUARDO GALEANO

Open Veins of Latin America

Memory of Fire:
Volume I, Genesis
Volume II, Faces and Masks
Volume III, Century of the Wind

The Book of Embraces

Soccer in Sun and Shadow

Upside Down

"In history, as in nature, decay is the laboratory of life."

— Karl Marx

Foreword by Sandra Cisneros

I have been in the company of the man I consider my teacher only a handful of times and always too briefly. In Boston we shared a stage. It was an old wooden theater, the kind where Lincoln might've been shot. There was no microphone, or if there was, it didn't work. I had to shout to be heard. I read as if I were angry. It was the only way. In the back of my head, it occurs to me Eduardo Galeano is listening to me, and this thought makes my blood freeze.

"My memory will save what is worthwhile. My memory knows more about me than I do. It doesn't lose what deserves to be saved."

In the spring of '91 while teaching in Albuquerque, I was asked if I would escort you for the day. You wanted to go to Acoma and needed a driver; you don't drive. I was such a devoted fan, if you had asked me to drive you back to Montevideo I would've said yes. It was a straight shot west to that mythical city high up on a mesa. Poor Eduardo! I chattered like a monkey the entire trip. You must've been exhausted. It's not half as tiring to talk as it is to listen.

I believe certain people, events, and books come to you when they must, at their precise moment in history. You arrived sent by "Saint Coincidence," as the poet Joy Harjo might say. Saint Coincidence led me first to *Memory of Fire* in '87. That was the year I wanted to die and did die, but Divine Providence resurrected me.

~

Once before I had met you at a book signing, but that was only briefly. The line meandered as sluggishly as the Rio Grande. When you finally came into view, I saw why. You talked to everyone. Everyone. Not chatter, but dialogue. Next to your name you drew little pictures of a pig and a daisy. You hugged people; some you even kissed!

Back then I made the mistake, as only the naive can, of confusing the books with the author. When I met you again this year, I'm happy to report, I was wiser.

The book is the sum of our highest potential. Writers, alas, are the rough drafts.

~

This time we spend the day driving around my city on a scavenger hunt of sorts, for various items you were asked to take back to Montevideo. One of them makes me laugh—a collapsible piñata, one that squashes down for easy transport and later can be opened and filled. You're certain we can find one if we only look. I haven't the heart to tell you there is no such thing except in the minds of poets and inventors.

~

When I read your work what I find remarkable is my inability to classify what I'm reading. Is this history? And if so, it seems to me to be the best kind, full of gossip, full of story. Your books read like fable, fairy tale, myth, poem, diary, journal, but certainly not the dull lines of historical writing. And then I understand. You're an acrobat, Eduardo. You're a storyteller.

~

You have a list of things to buy. We go to my favorite vintage shop where you buy nothing and you watch me buy everything. We stop at a supermarket to buy you cans of jalape, find CDs for your children, tequila for your agent, and a tailor to have your jeans hemmed. We eat breakfast tacos at Taqueria No Que No.

By your own admission you call yourself a chronicler, but this doesn't say exactly what you do, what you give to writers like me. We've traded stories of how difficult it is to write, and it's a great relief to hear someone else say how difficult it is to compose a short paragraph, to rewrite it thirty, forty times. It gives me *animo* to hear about how each book becomes more difficult for you. Because with each book your standards are raised.

Carranza's Meat Market is where we stop next for barbacoa Tex-Mex. It amuses you because of the railroad across the street. "What poetic justice," you say, "Mexican President Carranza was plagued by the Zapatistas bombing the railroads, and now here are the railroads across the street plaguing his descendants."

I think, when I look at you, how did you do it, remain human, after everything? What is left after so many goodbyes, after everything? After much pain, much fear?

I'm not a writer in exile. I've never been exiled from anything, except maybe a bar or two.

I can't imagine being in exile.

I look and can't find you in the books you write. You do a Sally Rand fan dance. I find you only in this book—*Days and Nights of Love and War*. Only here do I catch glimpses of you refracted in the mirror of other faces, dreams, stories of other dreamers, stories of other storytellers.

"I've known few people who have survived the tests of pain and violence—a rare feat—with their capacity for tenderness intact."

You don't talk about yourself, Eduardo. You talk about my house, about my dogs, about the book I am writing, and sometimes for a wisp of a moment you mention you. But only by inference.

On our way to the errands you say, "I didn't expect so many trees and hills here. San Antonio is very pleasant. It looks like a good town to walk in." "Oh, do you like to walk?" "I walk all the time," you say; "Blocks and blocks." And I try to imagine you walking through the streets of Montevideo, through Buenos Aires, through Calella de la Costa where you've written this book.

I imagine you walking through all the cities where you've lived exiled from your last life. I imagine you drinking in bars and eating as you do here with me, con gusto. I gather from sharing beer and food with you a little of who you are. I see you riding trains and buses. The waiter fills your glass with beer, a woman hands you change. People talk to you without knowing who you are. People like to talk to you because you like to listen. You are a writer, you are a witness.

~

You once told me a writer can write of life only if he has experienced death. You weren't talking about yourself, you rarely talk of you, but I thought of you and your first death at nineteen chronicled here. Your body was already in the morgue, until someone, "Saint Coincidence" perhaps, chanced to notice you were still breathing. Since this death and the subsequent deaths and resurrections, you write with life. One way to conquer death.

~

Your memory startles me. Your attention to detail. You quote poems as easily as you do history. On the ride to Acoma your face furrows into x's when you grill me about a short story of mine. "What did you mean here: 'I believe love is always eternal. Even if eternity is only five minutes.'?" And I explain myself. "Ah," you say. "Is that it?" Silence. Then you add: "You love like a man."

~

Love resuscitates the living dead, don't you think? For others, it is laughter. For writers, the pen is our savior. For some the needle, I suppose, or the bottle, or perhaps that rare elixir, poetry. I don't know how it is for others, for those without words, I mean. I can only imagine. For me, there are the writers like you, who remind me why I write.

"And what about love, Eduardo?"

"Love? The Brazilian poet Vins de Moraes says it best. *No es infinito pero es infinito en cuanto dura*. It's not infinite, but it's infinite while it lasts."

I make you write this down for me, and you do, adding your signature pig.

We walk into a shop full of piñatas. Hundreds of piñatas. Piñatas shaped like superheroes and cartoons, like soldiers and like chihuahuas, but no collapsible piñatas. At least you and I are in agreement. These piñatas are *bien feos*. The best kind is the old-fashioned piñata. The one shaped like a star.

You teach me to remain faithful to the word. To revere the syllable as a poet does, to remain attentive to writing as if one's life, several lives, depended upon it.

This is what I want. To believe one can write to change the world.

To change the world.

I do not believe, Eduardo, that you are as you claim, an atheist. You believe in "Saint Coincidence," the power of love, and in *brujos*: that religion called superstition by the unconverted and spirtuality by the devout. In short, you believe in humanity.

On that first visit to Albuquerque you had a hard time reading the English translations of your work. With one vignette in particular, you're obsessed with the English translation, how it doesn't ring as true as the original Spanish. "We have to revise it," you plead. You make me sit down with you at the Albuquerque airport and get to work. You insist. The little furrows on your forehead don't disappear until we've gone over the vignette and revised and revised and revised.

After hearing you speak, we don't sleep for days. Some of us want to write like you. Some of us want to be you. Our crush is laughable.

Television producers, journalists, university professors, cashiers, lesbian lawyers, dentists, opera singers, students, retired school teachers, nurses, gay painters, and straight architects. We are in love with your words, with the deep voice saying them, with the way you speak English, the way you speak Spanish.

Admiration is a love potion.

"I have known the machinery of terror from the inside and that exile has not always been easy. I could celebrate that at the end of so much sorrow and so much death, I still keep alive my capacity for astonishment at marvelous things, and my capacity for indignation at infamy, and that I continue to believe the advice of the poet who told me not to take seriously anything that does not make me laugh."

It's like the Last Supper. We're hanging on your every word. A table full of San Antonio artists and poets have come to the Liberty Bar to have an encore of Eduardo after his reading. A penniless painter pulls like a rabbit from a hat a gift he's made for you that evening. He had to run home to make it.

It's a collapsible piñata!

You're overjoyed! You laugh like a child. Greedy and grateful.

"I thought I knew some good stories to tell other people, and I discovered, or confirmed, that I had to write. I had often been convinced that this solitary trade wasn't worthwhile if you compare it, for example, to political activism or adventure. I had written and published a lot, but I hadn't the guts to dig down inside and open up and give of myself. Writing was dangerous, like making love the way one should."

Eduardo, I love your books because you write like a woman.

San Antonio de Béxar

DAYS AND NIGHTS OF LOVE AND WAR

The Windswept Face of the Pilgrim

Edda Armas told me, in Caracas, about her great grandfather. About what little was known, because the story began when he was already close to seventy and lived in a small town deep in the heart of the Clarines region. Apart from being old, poor, and ailing, her great grandfather was blind. And he married—no one knows how—a girl of eighteen.

Every now and then he would run away. He would, not she. He would run away from her and go to the road. There he would crouch down in the woods and wait for the sound of hoofs or of wheels. Then the blind man would walk out to the crossing and ask to be taken anywhere.

That is how his great granddaughter imagined him now: sitting astride the rump of a mule, roaring with laughter as he ambled down the road, or sitting in the back of a cart, covered with clouds of dust and joyfully dangling his bird's legs over the edge.

I Close My Eyes and Am in the Middle of the Sea

I lost quite a few things in Buenos Aires. Due to the rush or to bad luck, no one knows where they ended up. I left with a few clothes and a handful of papers.

I don't complain. With so many people lost, to cry over things is to lack respect for pain.

Gypsy life. Things are next to me but then they disappear. I have them by night, I lose them by day. I'm not a prisoner of things; they don't decide anything.

When I split up with Graciela, I left the house in Montevideo intact. The Cuban seashells and the Chinese swords, the Guatemalan tapestries, the records and the books and everything else. To have taken something would have been cheating. All this was hers, time shared, time I'm grateful for. And I set out for the unknown, clean and unburdened.

My memory will retain what is worthwhile. My memory knows more about me than I do; it doesn't lose what deserves to be saved.

Inner fever: cities and people, unattached to my memory, float toward me: land, where I was born, children I made, men and women who swelled my soul.

Buenos Aires, May 1975: Oil Is a Fatal Subject

– 1 –

Yesterday, near the Ezeiza airport, a journalist from *La Opinión* was found dead. His name was Jorge Money. His fingers were burnt and his fingernails pulled out.

In the magazine's editorial office Villar Araujo, biting his pipe, asked me, "And when will it be our turn?"

We laughed.

In the issue of *Crisis* now on the streets we published the last part of Villar's report on oil in Argentina. The article denounces the colonial statutes which govern oil contracts in the country today and it relates the history of the oil business, with its tradition of infamy and crime.

"When oil is involved," Villar writes, "accidental deaths don't occur." In October 1962, in a chalet in Bella Vista, Tibor Berény was shot three times, from different angles and in different parts of his body. According to the official report, this was a suicide. Berény was not, however, a contortionist, but a high-ranking advisor to Shell. He was also apparently a double or triple agent for U.S. firms. More recently, in February of this year, the body of Adolfo Cavalli was found. Cavalli, who had been a union leader for the oil workers, had fallen into disgrace. The loss of power had improved his thinking. Of late he had been preaching the virtues of the total nationalization of oil. He had, above all, a great deal of influence in military circles. When they riddled him with bullets in Villa Soldati, he had a briefcase in his hand. The briefcase disappeared. The press reported that the briefcase had been full of cash. Robbery had thus been the motive for the crime.

Villar ties these Argentine cases to other international murders that reek of oil. And he warns in his article, "If you, reader, discover that after writing these lines a bus ran over me as I crossed the street, think the worst and you will be right."

– 2 –

News. Villar waits for me in my office, quite excited. Someone has called him by phone and in a very nervous voice said that Cavalli's briefcase contained not money but documents.

"No one knows what documents these were. Just me. And I know because I gave them to him. I'm afraid. I want you to know too, Villar. The briefcase held . . ."

And at that moment, click, the line was cut.

– 3 –

Last night Villar Araujo did not return home to sleep.

– 4 –

We search high and low. The journalists go on strike. Newspapers from the provinces weren't out today. The minister has promised to look into this case personally. The police deny having any information. At the magazine we get anonymous phone calls, giving us contradictory information.

– 5 –

Villar Araujo reappeared last night, alive, on an empty road near Ezeiza. He was left there with four other people.

He had been given neither food nor drink for two days and his head had been covered by a hood. He had been interrogated about the sources for his articles, among other things. He saw only the shoes of his interrogators.

The federal police issued a communiqué about the affair. They say that Villar Araujo had been arrested by mistake.

Ten Years Ago I Attended the Dress Rehearsal of This Play

– 1 –

How many men will be yanked from their homes tonight and thrown into the wastelands with a few holes in their backs?

How many will be mutilated, blown up, burnt?

Terror stalks out of the shadows, strikes, and returns to the darkness. A woman's red eyes, an empty chair, a shattered door, someone who will not be back: Guatemala 1967, Argentina 1977.

That year had been officially declared the "year of peace" in Guatemala. But no one fished anymore near the city of Gualán because the nets brought up human bodies. Today the tide washes up pieces of cadavers on the banks of the Río de la Plata. Ten years ago bodies appeared in the Río Motagua or were found, at dawn, in gorges or roadside ditches: featureless faces which could never be identified. After the threats came the kidnappings, the attacks, the torture, the assassinations. The NOA (New Anticommunist Organization)—which proclaimed that it worked "together with the glorious army of Guatemala"—pulled out its enemies' tongues and cut off their left hands. The MANO (Organized Nationalist Anticommunist Movement), which worked with the police, placed black crosses on the doors of the condemned.

At the bottom of San Roque Lake, in Córdoba, Argentina, bodies sunk with rocks are now appearing, just as in the area surrounding the Pacaya Volcano, Guatemalan peasants found a cemetery full of rotting bones and bodies.

– 2 –

In the torture chambers the torturers eat lunch in front of their victims. Children are interrogated as to the whereabouts of their parents: the parents are strung up and given electric shocks so they will reveal the location of their children. Daily news item: "Individuals in civilian attire, faces covered by black hoods . . . They arrived in four Ford Falcons . . . They were all heavily armed, with pistols, machine guns, and Itakas . . . The first police arrived an hour after the killings." Prisoners, pulled out of jail, die "attempting to escape" in battles in which the army reports neither wounded nor killed on its side. Black humor in Buenos Aires: "Argentines," they say, "can be divided into the terrorized, the imprisoned, the buried, and the exiled." The death penalty was incorporated into the Penal Code in mid-1976, but each day people are killed in this country with benefit of neither trials nor sentences. The majority are deaths without bodies. The Chilean dictatorship has wasted no time in imitating this successful procedure. A single execution can unleash an international scandal: for thousands of disappeared people, there is always the benefit of the doubt. As in Guatemala, friends and relatives make the useless, dangerous pilgrimage from prison to prison, from barracks to barracks, while the bodies rot in the bushes or dumps. The technique of the "disappeared": there are no prisoners to claim nor martyrs to mourn. The earth devours the people and the government washes its hands. There are no crimes to denounce nor explanations to give. Each death dies over and over again until, finally, the only thing your soul retains is a mist of horror and uncertainty.

– 3 –

But Guatemala was the first Latin American laboratory in which the "dirty war" was carried out on a large scale. Men trained, guided, and armed by the United States implemented the extermination plan. The year 1967 was a long St. Bartholomew's Day massacre.[1]

The violence had begun in Guatemala years before, when, one late afternoon in June 1954, Castillo Armas' P-47s had filled the sky. Later the land was returned to the United Fruit Company and a new Petroleum Law, translated from the English, was passed.

In Argentina, the Triple A (Argentine Anticommunist Alliance) made its public debut in 1973. If in Guatemala the "dirty war" was unleashed to brutally stamp out the agrarian reform and then expanded to erase this reform from the memories of the landless peasants, in Argentina the horror began when Juan Domingo Perón, from the seat of power, dashed the hopes he had raised among the people during his long exile. Black humor in Buenos Aires: "Power," they say, "is like a violin. It is held by the left hand and played by the right." Afterward, at the end of the summer of 1976, the military returned to the presidential palace. Wages are now worth half of what they were. The unemployed have multiplied. Strikes are banned. The universities have been returned to the Middle Ages. The big multinational firms have regained control over fuel distribution, bank deposits, and the sale of meat and grains. New trial legislation allows legal disputes between multinational firms and Argentina to be handled in foreign courts. The foreign investment law has been eliminated: the multinationals can take away whatever they please now.

Aztec ceremonies are held in Argentina. To which blind god is so much blood offered? Can this program be imposed on Latin America's best organized workers' movement without paying the price of five cadavers a day?

The Universe As Seen Through a Keyhole

Valeria asks her father to turn the record over. She explains that "Arroz con Leche" lives on the other side.

Diego chats with his friend inside him, whose name is Andrés, and who is a skeleton.

Fanny explains how today her friend was drowned in the river at school, which is very deep, and that from down there below everything was transparent and you could see the feet of grownups, the soles of their shoes.

Claudio grabs one of Alejandra's fingers. "Lend me your finger," he says, and he sinks it in the can of milk on the burner, because he wants to see if it is too hot.

From the other room Florencia calls me and asks me if I can touch my nose with my bottom lip.

Sebastian suggests we escape in a plane, but he warns me to watch out for the lights and the propeller.

Mariana, on the terrace, pushes the wall, which is her way of helping the earth to rotate.

Patricio holds the lit match between his fingers and his son blows and blows the little flame that will never go out.

Are Any of the Boys I Met Back Then in the Mountains Still Alive?

— 1 —

They were very young. City students and peasants from country provinces where a liter of milk costs two full days of labor. The army was on their tail and they told dirty jokes and roared with laughter.

I spent a few days with them. We ate tortillas. The nights were quite cold in the high Guatemalan jungles. We slept on the ground, hugging one another, bodies glued together for warmth and to keep the early morning freeze from killing us.

— 2 —

There were a few Indians among the guerrillas. Almost all the enemy soldiers were Indians. The army nabbed them when their festivals ended. When the effect of liquor wore off they were already in uniform and carrying guns. And then they marched off into the mountains, to kill those who died for them.

— 3 —

One night the boys told me how Castillo Armas had rid himself of a dangerous aide. To prevent this man from robbing him of power or women, Castillo Armas sent him on a secret mission to Managua. He carried a sealed letter for the dictator Somoza.

Somoza received him in the palace. He opened the letter, read it to himself in front of the bearer, and said,

"What your president requests shall be done."

They drank together.

At the end of a long, pleasant chat, Somoza accompanied him to the door. Suddenly Castillo Armas' emissary found himself alone, with the door shut behind him.

The firing squad, already in formation, awaited him. The soldiers all fired at once.

— 4 —

Conversation I either heard or imagined during those days:

"A revolution from sea to sea. The whole country up in arms. And I intend to see it with my own eyes . . ."

"And will everything, everything change?"

"To the roots."

"And we'll no longer have to work for nothing?"

"Of course not."

"Nor put up with being treated like animals?"

"No one will own anyone else."

"And the rich?"

"There won't be any more rich."

"And then who is going to pay the poor for their crops?"

"There won't be any more poor. Don't you see?"

"No rich, no poor."

"No poor, no rich."

"But Guatemala won't have any more people then. Because here, you know, whoever isn't rich is poor."

— 5 —

The vice president was named Clemente Marroquín Rojas. He ran a rather bombastic newspaper, and at his office door two fat men carrying machine guns kept guard.

Marroquín Rojas greeted me with an embrace. He offered me coffee, he slapped my back and looked at me with tenderness.

I, who had been in the mountains with the guerrillas until the week before, didn't understand anything. "It's a trap," I thought, for the pleasure of thinking myself important.

Then Marroquín Rojas explained that Newbery, the brother of the famous Argentine aviator, had been his great friend during his youth and that I was his spitting image. He forgot he was in the presence of a journalist. Transformed into Newbery, I listened as he ranted against the Americans, because they didn't do things properly. A squadron of U.S. planes, flown by U.S. pilots, had left Panama and dropped napalm over a mountain in Guatemala. Marroquín Rojas was furious because the planes had returned to Panama without touching Guatemalan soil.

"They could have landed, don't you think?" he asked, and I agreed.

"They could have landed, at the very least."

– 6 –

I had heard it from the guerrillas.

Several times they had seen napalm explode in the sky above neighboring mountains. They had often discovered the foam's red hot footprints: trees scorched to the roots, animals burnt to a crisp, rocks blackened.

– 7 –

In mid-1954 the United States had placed Ngo Dinh Diem on the throne in Saigon and had arranged the triumphal entry of Castillo Armas in Guatemala.

With one stroke, the rescue expedition for the United Fruit Company cut through the agrarian reform which had expropriated the uncultivated land of this company and distributed it among landless peasants.

My generation began its political life with that mark on its forehead. Hours of indignation and of impotence. . . . I remember the corpulent orator who spoke to us with a serene voice while at the same time spitting fire from his mouth, that night of angry shouts and banners in Montevideo. "We have come to denounce the crime ..."

The speaker's name was Juan José Arévalo. I was fourteen years old and the impact of that moment never was to fade.

Arévalo had begun in Guatemala the cycle of social reforms which Jacobo Arbenz was to extend and which Castillo Armas drowned in blood.

During his government, he told us, he had survived thirty-two coup attempts.

Years later Arévalo became a government functionary. A dangerous species, the repentant: Arévalo became an ambassador under General Araña, feudal lord, colonial administrator of Guatemala, organizer of the butchery.

When I learned this, I had long since lost my innocence, but I felt like a cheated little boy.

– 8 –

I met Mijangos in 1967 in Guatemala. He received me in his home, no questions asked, when I came down from the mountains to the city.

He liked to sing, to drink good liquor, to embrace life. He had no legs for dancing, but he clapped his hands to liven up parties.

A while later, when Arévalo was ambassador, Adolfo Mijangos was a congressman.

One afternoon, Mijangos denounced a fraud in congress. The Hanna Mining Company, which had toppled two governments in Brazil, had succeeded in making a company official Guatemala's economics minister. A contract was shortly signed whereby Hanna would exploit, in partnership with the state, the nickel, cobalt, copper, and chrome deposits on the shores of Lake Izabal. According to the agreement, the state would be paid a tip for its efforts while the company would get over a billion dollars. In its role as the country's partner, Hanna would pay no income taxes and would be able to make use of the port at half price.

Mijangos lifted his voice in protest.

Shortly thereafter, when he was getting into his Peugeot, a round of bullets riddled his back. He fell from his wheelchair, his body full of lead.

– 9 –

Hidden in a store in the suburbs, I awaited the man most wanted by Guatemala's military police. His name was Ruano Pinzón, and he too was, or had been, in the military police.

"Look at this wall. Jump. Can you?"

I craned my neck. The wall behind the store stretched up and up.

"No," I said.

"But if they come, will you jump?"

Nothing else to do. If they came, I would fly. Panic turns anyone into an Olympic champion.

But they didn't come. Ruano Pinzón came that night and I was able to talk with him at length. He wore a black leather jacket and his nerves made his eyes dance. Ruano Pinzón had deserted.

He was the only living witness to the killing of some twenty political leaders on the eve of the elections.

It had taken place in the Matamoros barracks. Ruano Pinzón was one of the four police who had carried the large, heavy bags to the trucks. He noticed because his sleeves became soaked in blood. At Aurora airport they lifted the bags into an Air Force "500." Later, they dumped them into the Pacific.

He had seen them arrive at the barracks, badly beaten up, and he had seen the defense minister personally commanding the operation.

Of the men who had carried the bodies, Ruano Pinzón was the only one left. One of the men had been found in a bed in the "Pensión La Posada" one morning with a knife in his chest. Another had been shot through the back in a bar in Zacapa, and the other had been shot down in a bar behind the central station.

Why Do the Doves Cry at Dawn?

Because one night a male and a female dove went to a dance, the male was killed, in a fight, by someone who held a grudge against him. The party was lovely and the female didn't want to stop having a good time. "Tonight I'll sing," she said, "and in the morning I'll cry." And when the sun rose on the horizon she cried.

This is how I was told it by Malena Aguilar, who had been told it by her grandmother, a woman of gray eyes and a wolf nose, who at night, by the heat of the coal stove, bewitched her grandchildren with stories of haunting ghosts and slit throats.

The Tragedy Had Been a True Prophecy

— I —

In mid-1973 Juan Domingo Perón returned to Argentina after eighteen years of exile.

It was the largest political demonstration in the entire history of Latin America. In the fields near Ezeiza airport and all along the highway, more than 2 million people had gathered, with children and drums and guitars, from all parts of the country. The people, with long-lasting patience and an iron will, had recovered their *caudillo* and they returned him to his land with a royal welcome.

The mood was festive. The people's happiness, contagious beauty, embraced me, lifted me up, gave me faith. My eyes still retained the image of the Broad Front's torches as they weaved along the avenues of Montevideo.[2] Now, in the outskirts of Buenos Aires, gathered together in a gigantic, borderless campsite, were the older workers for whom Peronism was a vivid memory of dignity, and the young people, who had not lived through the experiences of 1946 and 1955, and for whom Peronism was constructed more out of hope than nostalgia.

The party ended in a massacre. At Ezeiza, in one afternoon, more Peronists were killed than during the years of resistance against the previous military dictatorships. "And now, who should we hate?" asked the stupefied people. The ambush had been planned by Peronists against Peronists. Peronism had its Tyrians and its Trojans, its workers and its bosses; and within this scenario real history unfolded as a continuous contradiction.

The union bureaucrats, the political bosses, and the agents of those in power had revealed their bankruptcy in the fields near Ezeiza. Like the king in the story, they appeared naked before the public eye. The professional killers then stepped in to take the place of the people.

The merchants, briefly expelled from the temple, reentered through the rear door.

What happened at Ezeiza was a preview of what would come later. The government of Héctor Cámpora was short-lived as a lily.[3] After that, the promises lagged behind reality, until they dropped out of sight altogether. Sad epilogue to a popular movement. "God has prestige because he shows so little of himself," Perón had told me, years before in Madrid. Salaries increased, but this just proved that the workers were responsible for the crisis. A cow soon was worth less than a pair of shoes. And while the small and medium-sized manufacturers went under, the oligarchy, undefeated, displayed itself in rags and gave vent to its anger through the newspapers, radio, and television. The agrarian reform proved to be worth less than the paper on which it was written, and the loopholes remained open through which the wealth generated by the country could—and still does—drain out. Those in power in Argentina, as all over Latin America, tuck their fortunes safely away in Zurich or New York. There the money performs a circus trick, returning to the country magically converted into very expensive international loans.

– 2 –

Can national unity be obtained above, through, and despite the class struggle? Perón had given body to this collective illusion.

One morning, during the first days of exile, the *caudillo* had explained to his host in Asunción, Paraguay, the political importance of the smile.

"Do you want to see my smile?" he had asked.

And he put his false teeth in the palm of his hand.

During the course of eighteen years, for or against him, Argentine politics revolved around this man. The successive military coups were no more than tributes which fear paid to the truth: given free elections, Peronism would win. Everything depended upon Perón's blessings and curses, thumbs up, thumbs down, and from the letters he wrote from far away, with the left hand or with the right, giving ever contradictory orders to the men who risked their lives.

In Madrid in the fall of 1966 Perón told me:

"Do you know how the Chinese kill sparrows? They don't let them rest on tree branches. They harass them with sticks and don't let them land, until the birds die in the air; their hearts give out, and they fall to the ground. Traitors fly like sparrows. It's enough to harass them, to prevent them from resting, to bring them down. No, No ... To lead men you have to fly like an eagle, not a sparrow. Leading men is a technique, an art. It requires military precision. You have to let the traitors fly, but without letting them rest. And wait for Providence to do its work. You must let Providence act ... Especially because I control Providence."

When the time came, when Peronism returned to power, it fell to pieces. It disintegrated slowly before the *caudillo* died.

– 3 –

José Luis Nell was one of the victims of the Ezeiza massacre. A bullet shattered his spinal column. He was paralyzed.

One day he decided to put an end to the impotence and the pity.

He picked the date and the place: an overpass at a train station where no trains passed. Someone took him there in his wheelchair and placed the loaded pistol in his hand.

José Luis had been an iron-willed militant. He had survived bullets and jails and the years of hunger and clandestinity.

But now he put the barrel in his mouth and pulled the trigger.

Dreams

Our entwined bodies change position while we sleep, shifting this way and that. Your head on my chest, my thigh on your belly, and as our bodies turn, the bed turns and the room and the world turn. "No, No," you explain, thinking you are awake. "We are no longer there. We moved to another country while we slept."

A Flash That Lingers on Between the Eyebrows

It happened that afternoon, on the platform, as I waited for the train to Barcelona.

The light kindled the earth between the ties. Suddenly the earth took on a vivid color, as if blood had rushed to its head, and it swelled up under the blue tracks.

I wasn't happy, but the earth was while that long moment lasted, and it was I who had the awareness to know it and the memory to recall it.

Tale of the Hunted Man and the Night Lady

They meet, in the early hours, at a posh bar. The next morning he wakes up in her bed. She makes coffee; they drink it from the same cup. He discovers that she bites her fingernails and has lovely little-girl hands. They don't talk. While he dresses, he searches for the words to explain that he can't pay her. Without looking at him she says, as if in an aside,

"I don't know what your name is. But if you want to stay here, stay. The house isn't bad."

And he stays.

She asks no questions. Neither does he.

At night, she goes out to work. He rarely leaves the house.

The months roll by.

Early one morning she encounters an empty bed. On the pillow a letter says,

"I wanted to take one of your hands with me. I stole a glove. Forgive me. Good-bye and a thousand thanks for everything."

He crosses the river with falsified papers. A few days later he is arrested in Buenos Aires. He is caught as a result of an absurd coincidence. They had been hunting for him for over a year.

The colonel insults and beats him. He lifts him up by his collar.

"You're going to tell us where you were. You're going to tell us everything."

He answers that he lived with a woman in Montevideo. The colonel doesn't believe him. He shows the photograph: the woman sitting on the bed, naked, with her hands on her neck, her long black hair slipping down over her breasts.

"With this woman," he says. "In Montevideo."

The colonel grabs the snapshot from his hand and, suddenly enraged, bangs a fist on the table and yells, "That bitch, that motherfucking traitor, she's going to pay for this. She is really going to pay for this."

And then he realizes. Her home had been a trap, set up to catch men like him. And he remembered what she had told him, one noon, after they had made love.

"You know something? I never felt, with anyone else, this ... this joy in my muscles."

And for the first time he understands what she had added, with a rare shadow in her eyes.

"It had to happen to me someday, didn't it?" she had said. "I know how to lose."

(This happened in 1956 or 1957, when Argentines who were hunted down by the dictatorship in that country crossed the river and hid in Montevideo.)

The Universe as Seen Through a Keyhole

Elsa and Ale sat side by side in class. At recess they walked hand in hand around the schoolyard. They shared homework, secrets, and pranks.

One morning Elsa said she had spoken to her dead grandmother.

Since then her grandmother had often sent them messages. Every time Elsa ducked her head underwater, she heard her grandmother's voice.

After a time Elsa announced,

"Grandmother says we're going to fly."

They tried it in the schoolyard and in the street. They ran around in circles or in straight lines until they collapsed in exhaustion. They had several bad falls jumping from the railings.

Elsa dunked her head and her grandmother told her, "You are going to fly during the summer."

Vacation time arrived. The girls' families went to different beaches.

At the end of February Elsa returned with her parents to Buenos Aires. She made the car stop in front of a house she had never seen before.

Ale opened the door.

"Did you fly?" Elsa asked.

'"No," Ale said.

"I didn't either," Elsa said.

They hugged each other, crying.

Buenos Aires, July 1975: Returning from the South

Carlos had gone far away. He had been a hotel cook, beach photographer, occasional reporter, man without a home; he had vowed never to return to Montevideo.

He is in Buenos Aires now, without a cent to his name and carrying a tattered and expired identification card.

We owe each other many words. We go to the coast on the weekend to catch up.

I remember having listened, with childlike awe, twenty years ago, to the stories of his wanderings as a jack of all trades around the eastern rice fields and the sugarcane plantations of northern Uruguay. I had felt myself to be a friend of this man for the first time. It had been in the Tupé Nambá cafe off Plaza Independencia. He had a guitar with him. He was a minstrel and a poet, born in San José.

Over the years he earned a reputation as a troublemaker. After his return from Paraguay he got drunk often. He spent a year locked up in a concentration camp in the Tacumbú quarry: the scars from chain lashes on his back never faded. They had pulled out his eyebrows and mustache with a knife. Every Sunday the soldiers ran races astride the prisoners, who wore bits and everything, while the priest sipped tea under an ombú tree and clutched his belly with laughter.

Tough and quiet, Carlos was hard on himself and with his eyes searched out enemies in the cafes and bars of Montevideo. At the same time, he was the delight of my children. No one was better at telling stories and nonsense and not a clown in the world was as able as he to make them roll on the floor in laughter. Carlos came to our house, put on an apron, and cooked chicken à la portuguesa or dishes he concocted for our pleasure, because he was not a big eater himself.

Now we were returning from the coast, headed for Buenos Aires, several hours on the bus without sleep and talking and he spoke about Montevideo. During the entire weekend neither of us had mentioned our city. We couldn't go there; it was better to remain silent.

On a sad note, he told me about Pacha.

"One night I came home quite late and lay down without making noise or turning on the light. Pacha wasn't in bed. I looked for her in the bathroom and in the room where her son slept. She wasn't there. I found the dining room door closed. I went to open it and I realized: on the other side of the door there were blankets on the floor. The next morning I waited for her in the kitchen, to drink *mate* with her as usual. Pacha didn't say anything. Neither did I. We chatted a bit, the usual—the nice or lousy weather and the tough political situation shaping up or please pass the *mate* and I'll turn over the tea so it doesn't get washed out. And when I returned at night I found the bed empty. Again the dining room door was closed. I put my ear to it and thought I could hear her breathing. Early the next morning we sat in the kitchen to drink *mate.* She didn't say anything and I didn't ask. At 8:30 her students arrived, as usual. And that's how it was for a week: the bed without her in it, the door closed. Until early one morning, when she passed me the last *mate,* I said, "Look Pacha. I know it is very uncomfortable to sleep on the floor. So tonight just go to the bed. I won't be there." And I never went back.

It Is the Time for Ghosts: I Call Them, Pursue Them, Catch Them

I draw them with dirt and blood on the cave ceiling. I look within myself with the eyes of the first man. While the ceremony lasts, I feel that in my memory the entire history of the world can fit, starting with that first chap who rubbed two stones together to get warmed by the first little fire.

The System

I was fourteen or fifteen years old and worked as a messenger in a bank. I spent all afternoon running up and down stairs with mountains of files in my arms. I stood in a corner, like a little soldier, at the beck and call of bells, lights, and voices.

The board of directors of the bank met on Fridays, on the top floor. During the meetings the directors would have coffee several times. I ran to the kitchen to make the coffee. If there was no one around I would boil it, to give them diarrhea.

One Friday I came in with the tray, as usual, and found the big room nearly empty. Neatly placed on the mahogany table were the files bearing the names of each director, and around the table sat the empty chairs. Only Sr. Alcorta was seated at his place. I offered him coffee and he didn't reply. He had put his glasses on and was reading a piece of paper. He read it several times. Standing quietly behind him, I looked at the rolls of pink flesh around his neck and counted the freckles on his hands. The letter was the text of his resignation. He signed it, took off his glasses and remained seated, his hands in his pockets, staring into space. I coughed. I coughed again, but I didn't exist. My arms were getting cramps from holding the tray full of coffee cups.

When I returned to pick up the files and take them to the Secretariat, Sr. Alcorta had gone. I locked the door and opened the files, as I always did, one by one. In each file there was a letter of resignation just like the one Sr. Alcorta had read and reread and signed. All the letters had been signed.

The following Tuesday the board of directors held a special meeting. Sr. Alcorta was not invited. The directors resolved, unanimously: first, to withdraw the resignations presented the previous Friday; and second, to accept Sr. Alcorta's resignation, thanking him for the services rendered and lamenting that new obligations were making demands on his invaluable abilities.

I read the resolutions in the minutes book when they told me to take it up to the General Manager's office.

The System

. . . that the computer program that alarms the banker who alerts the ambassador who dines with the general who summons the president who intimidates the minister who threatens the director general who humiliates the manager who yells at the boss who insults the employee who scorns the worker who mistreats his wife who beats the child who kicks the dog.

The System

We walk along the Barcelona boulevards, fresh tunnels of summer, and we draw up to a stall where birds are sold.

There are cages for one and for several birds. Adoum explains that in one-bird cages a little mirror is placed inside so the birds won't know they are alone.

Later, at lunch, Guaysamín talks about New York. He says he has seen men there drink by themselves at counters. That behind the row of bottles there is a mirror and sometimes, late at night, the men throw their glasses and the mirror shatters to bits.

Tale of the Burro of Vovô Catarino and How St. George Came Galloping Up on His White Horse and Saved Him from the Devil

– 1 –

The cars sported plastic stickers bearing the national colors and the slogan, "Brazil: No One Can Beat You." Pelé was already a bank director. Outside the cities beggars surrounded tourist buses. Dodge Dart promised in its advertising campaign: "You will become a member of the ruling class." Gillette said, "Brazil, I trust you." The death squads' mutilated victims turned up in the Baixada Fluminense. Their faces were shot up and their fingers severed so that they wouldn't be recognized. DuPont, Dow Chemical, Shell, and Standard Oil cried out from pages and screens, "We Believe in Brazil." In the slums, children slept on the floor or in cardboard boxes. From there, they watched the television bought on credit. The upper class played statistics, the middle class the stock market, the lower class bet on sports. Who would wake up a millionaire on Monday morning? An unemployed construction worker, a washerwoman, a shoeshine boy. Someone would be the chosen one. Someone, among the 80 million condemned in this land, would be picked by God on Monday morning.

– 2 –

I slept at Artur Poerner's.

Television studios were a few blocks away from the house. Every Sunday afternoon the contest candidates filled the street: Who can eat the most bananas in an hour? Which Brazilian has the longest nose? Once a crowd of midgets gathered and eyed one another loathingly. A fortune awaited the smallest midget in Brazil.

Another time there was a championship of the wretched. The court of miracles paraded: prostitutes since the age of eight, invalids abandoned by their children, people blinded as a result of hunger or blows, lepers, syphilitics, prisoners with life sentences for crimes they hadn't committed, children whose ears had been bitten off by rats, women who had been tied to bedposts for years. Fairytale prizes were promised to the most wretched of the wretched. Some brought along their own cheering section to the station. The fans got delirious, just like at soccer matches: "He's won! He's won!" the people in the audience would yell.

In the evenings at Artur's house we would hear the beating of drums. The tam-tam, rhythm of fever and thunder, came from Corcovado. From the top of the hill Christ protected the city with his arms. In the wooded hillside savage masses were held. The vengeful ghosts brought to this earth, by mood and firelight, the Paradise promised by the prophets.

– 3 –

Outside, Exile: little houses made of four sheets of tin and two planks hung on the mountains, blankets made of newspaper, children with swollen bellies, pin-thin legs, frightened eyes.

Inside, the Kingdom: the fire burned on the dirt floor and the drums sounded: men and women swayed, dreamed awake, beat at the doors of love or of death.

Artur and I enter, and find the Devil dressed in rags.

"Why do I want salvation?"

The cloth horns fell over his eyes. He jumped up and down on a heap of burning glass, his thorns of bottlenecks and garbage, and he banged the ground with an iron pitchfork.

"I don't want salvation!" came the hoarse voice from the fire. "It's nice in Hell. Hell is my home. And there, no one can give me orders."

The priestesses, dressed in red, sang,

"El sol ya viene,
ya viene, bahiano.
El sol ya va,
bahiano, ya va."

["The sun is about to come,
about to come, Bahian.
The sun is about to go,

Bahian, about to go."]

There were two altars in the *terreiro* [cult center] of Our Lady of the Conception, mother of Êxu: in the altar devoted to heavenly deities, a black Saint George rode forth on horseback; in the altar devoted to Satanic deities, weak candlelight scratched at skeletons and pitchforks.

"The ocean waves beat ...

The Devil ceremony was the shantytown's party.

"*Sem feitiço a vida não da pé, não da, não da.*" ["Without witchcraft, you can't get by, you can't get by."]

Vovô Catarino rubbed a live rooster—black feathers, red feathers—against the legs of a luckless suitor.

"Think about her."

He sharpened a new knife on the altar stone. Slowly he pulled the feathers from the rooster's neck. He raised his knife.

"Think about the girl."

The newly slit throat swelled and contracted. The suitor opened his mouth and drank.

"Tonight," announced Vovô, "there will be a bloodstain on her sheet. It won't be blood from a wound or from menstruation."

– 4 –

An old woman had been waiting her turn since the afternoon.

"Who's your boss?"

"A war hero."

"I asked his name."

"Charles Mann."

"That name isn't from these parts."

"He comes from a place called the United States."

"And how did he end up in Brazil?"

"His ship sank and he came here."

"What kind of hero is he, to run away?"

"He has lots of medals."

"A shit-faced hero, that's what he is."

"Don't say that, Vovô. My boss is an admiral."

"Bathtub admiral."

"But Vovô. He lost an eye in the war. He has one glass eye."

"When the black man ruins his sight," said Vovô, "he loses an eye. But a rich white man buys a glass eye. And you know what happens to him? He leaves the glass eye in a cup while he sleeps. And one morning he drinks water and swallows the glass eye. And the glass eye plugs up his ass and he looks out from his ass."

There is an outburst of drums and laughter. Tomé enjoyed himself as well: the ceremony was going nicely. Tomé was a fat goat, dressed as Êxu, who smoked cigars and played the drum with his horns. They had brought him in to be sacrificed and Vovô had taken a liking to him. Now he ruled over the ceremonies: when he butted into walls or people, Vovô understood that something was going wrong and he would leave.

– 5 –

With red chalk and black chalk Vovô drew the signs of Êxu on the dirt floor. He sprinkled powder; there was an explosion of white smoke.

"The sickness enters through the foot and through the foot it leaves," said Eunice, Vovô's priestess. "Although sometimes it enters through the mouth, when the neighbor sends a poisoned cake."

The sick man, with a colorless face, swollen stomach, and elephant feet, was burning with fever. His brothers had pushed him up the hill themselves. They had brought along a bottle of firewater.

Vovô got furious.

"When I say bring a bottle, that means bring seven. Do you want a cheap saint?"

He examined the man and diagnosed:

"Prepare the shroud. This spell was done very well."

– 6 –

Vovô raised his fist against God, calling him executioner and butcher, but at heart he knew he was a colleague.

"Why such sorrow?"

The black woman lifted her tear-streaked face. She had an enormous belly.

"You don't have a child there," Vovô proclaimed. "You have twenty. Twentuplets."

But she didn't laugh.

"Why such sadness, *minha filha?*"

"For my child, Vovô."

"For the twenty you have there?"

"I know my baby will be born dead."

"How?"

"I do, Vovô."

"Who told you such nonsense?"

"No one told me, but I know. My neighbor made a pact. She hates me. She wants to take my husband from me. She made a pact so my son will be born dead."

"And who did she make the pact with?"

"With God."

"With who?"

Vovô laughed, holding his belly.

"With God, Vovô."

"No, *minha filha,*" said Vovô, "with the Devil. God is not so dumb as to do that."

– 7 –

Before dawn, Vovô Catarino returned to the depths of Hell.

At night he would return to earth; he entered through his Burro's foot and he was doctor and clown, prophet and revenge-seeker of the shantytown. The man who received him in his body, Vovô's Burro, by day worked cleaning airplanes at the Galeão airport.

Artur and I walked up the slopes of the Corcovado. At dusk we would chat with the Burro, a soft and humble man, who served us coffee. At midnight we drank cane brandy or wine from Vovô's glass. We attended the trances and the sacrifices and we heard him scoff at institutions and good conduct.

He had different voices and different names for us. The Burro called Artur "carioca" and me "Uruguayo"; to Vovô we were "Curiboca" and "Furagaio." Vovô spoke with the hoarse and tangled voice of his thousands of years of age, and the Burro remembered nothing that Vovô said and did through him.

On the eve of my departure, and without my requesting it, Vovô gave me a good-luck necklace. He placed the tin chain on me as if arming a knight: I knelt on the ground and raised my head. A drum was played, voices sang.

The chain encircled my chest. For a year no bullets or hardships would enter it.

– 8 –

Eunice's daughter, Roxana, was just a few days old when she became consumed by fever. The baby cried continuously and refused food. Eunice wrapped her up and walked up the hill to Vovô's *terreiro.*

"She's dying," Eunice said.

"No."

They walked into the woods. Vovô baptized Roxana with two small knife cuts on her forehead. He made her his granddaughter. Afterward he threw twelve white roses down the waterfall, so the waterfall would take the disease out to sea.

After that, Eunice joined the *terreiro*.

– 9 –

She told me the story of the Burro and of Vovô.

The Burro was a tramp. He was living with other vagabonds under a bridge. One night they were so hungry they caught a rat, roasted and ate it. The Burro felt something strange in his body and fainted. He woke up transformed into Vovô Catarino. He said,

"Now I am going to help everyone. I am thousands of years old. To come to this world, I chose the person who was suffering most.

And then he began to sing.

"Vovô doesn't treat the Burro well," Eunice said. "Above all during Lent, Vovô loves to do mischief during Lent."

Vovô made him work so hard that the Burro didn't sleep. Moreover, Eunice told me, he made him drink urine during the ceremonies.

One fine day the Burro rebelled.

"I am not a dog to be leading this life. I cut myself and I burn my ass and I drink piss in exchange for hunger and bananas. I'm not going to do anything else for anybody. They can die for all I care."

As he finished speaking he felt dizzy. A voice whispered in his ear, "The problem is that you haven't had anything to eat, sir. Not even for breakfast. Let's go to a cafe to have something. Come on."

Vovô was going to cross the street when he fell backward violently. He reached out with his arm to get up and he fell again. He tried to lean on his hand and zap, again. The blows smashed his nose and gashed his head. He returned to the hill, bleeding and furious.

"Let's hope he doesn't try to come down to earth today. I'm not going to pay any more attention to that worthless Vovô."

He finished speaking and he fell down, struck by lightning. He remained there, face down. He couldn't move because of the pain. He cried.

Then Ogum, Saint George, the warrior saint, came down and picked him up by the armpits. It was strange that he should come on a Tuesday, because when Saint George came it was usually on a Friday night.

The Burro told him everything and asked for his help. Saint George is the only one the Devil listens to.

That night Vovô drank wine and cane brandy. Never again did he demand piss.

"Sometimes," Eunice told me, "the Burro deserves to be punished, because he disobeys."

The Burro was arranging the altars, while preparing to go to his job at the airport, when he discovered a glass of wine. Vovô had left it there to tempt him. The Burro could only drink during ceremonies, when he was Vovô. He had a sip and got a tremendous punch in the mouth. Two teeth fell out.

He walked down the hill to take the bus and ran into a funeral carriage. The carriage stopped. The Burro heard someone calling him. No sooner had he drawn near than they grabbed him by the neck, covered his mouth, and tossed him inside. He was in the land of death for three days and three nights. Saint George pulled him out of there. He swept him up on his galloping white horse and took him back home.

– 10 –

Carlos Widmann, foreign correspondent, asked me to take him to Vovô's *terreiro* so he could write an article. I was about to leave Rio and didn't have time, but I left him my contacts.

Later, in Montevideo, I got a letter from Widmann.

He said that on Good Friday he had been at Vovô Catarino's. Several black goats had been roasted and eaten that day of obligatory fasting. The ceremony had lasted until the next morning. Tomé had attended, smoking, the sacrifice of his brothers. The goats had their throats slit slowly, so they would suffer all the pain that God reserves for us humans, and they would thus relieve us of it. The guests had drunk the hot blood from cupped hands.

They had finished the goats when Vovô got a giant frog drunk on firewater. Each of the devout had placed the name or picture of his or her enemy in the frog's mouth. The frog slipped from Vovô's hand. Afterward he had sewed up the frog's mouth with unused needles. Red thread and black thread, in a cross. He released the frog at the door, and it hopped crazily away.

I knew that this meant slow death. The frog died of hunger. If a fast death is desired for the enemy, the frog is buried in a small coffin at the foot of a fig tree, the tree cursed by Christ, and the frog dies of suffocation.

"Vovô asked me to put in a name," Carlos wrote, "and I couldn't think of any. But I had just returned from Bolivia. I had very vivid memories of the massacres of miners. So I wrote the name of General René Barrientos on a slip of paper, I folded it up and put it in the frog's mouth."

When I read Widmann's letter, the Bolivian dictator had already been burnt alive in the Cañadón del Arque, swallowed up by the flames of a helicopter that had been given to him by Gulf Oil Company.

Introduction to Theology

During those days I discovered María Padilha.

She had been born in the rough section of Rio, and in a few years had invaded the poor neighborhoods in the northern part of the city.

She was the size of a woman.

She wore silk stockings and a very short skirt, with a slit that revealed her garter and laid bare her thighs, and a tight blouse, half open, from which her breasts bounced. She was covered with bracelets and necklaces showered upon her by her faithful. Between her long, red-nailed fingers she raised a filtertip, light tobacco cigarette.

María Padilha's wax figure guarded the doors of the shops where ceremonial items were sold. But where she really lived was in the bodies of the priestesses of the *terreiros*. María Padilha entered these women and from inside them she roared with laughter, drank, smoked, received consultations, gave advice, righted wrongs, and was even able to seduce the Devil to get him to help those who needed his help.

María Padilha, cursed goddess, deified whore, was incarnated in women who in *real* life were professional whores. They incarnated themselves, in a sense, but the other way around. Each ceremony was a ritual of dignity: "They thought I was a bitch? I'm a goddess."

All of This No Longer Exists

Many shantytowns have been removed from Rio. They have been thrown far away from the eyes of the tourists.

With them have gone their gods. The drums that beat out curses or give help no longer disturb the sleep of citizens.

The police closed Vovô Catarino's *terreiro*. They kicked him out of the city.

Introduction to Theology

– 1 –

Seven years ago I was slowly crossing the cold plaza in Llallaguea [Bolivia], my hands sunk in a black jacket with a high collar.

"Padre! Padrecito!"

A man came running up to me out of the darkness. He grabbed my arm. By the dim glow of the only street light, anyone could read the desperation in that bony face. He was wearing his miner's helmet and jacket. His voice sounded hoarse.

"You have to come with me, Father. I beg you."

I explained that I wasn't a priest. I explained it several times. It was useless.

"You have to come, padrecito, you have to come."

I fervently wanted to become a priest, if only for a few minutes. The miner's son was dying.

"It's the youngest, Father. You have to come and give him the last rites. Now, Father. He's leaving us."

He dug his fingers into my arm.

– 2 –

There are few children in the Bolivian mines. And there are no old men.

The men here are condemned to die before the age of thirty-five, their lungs reduced to cardboard by silica powder.

God alone is not enough.

Before, Lucifer himself opened the mining carnival. He entered, mounted on a white horse, and rode down the main street of Oruro. Today, the Devil festival attracts throngs of tourists from all over the world. But in the mines, the Devil does not reign in February alone. The miners call him "Tío" and they have made a throne in each shaft for him. The Tío is the true owner of the mine: he supplies or denies veins of tin, arranges that those he wants to destroy get lost in the labyrinth, or reveals hidden veins to his favorite sons. He thwarts or causes cave-ins. Inside the shaft it is fatal to pronounce the name Jesus, although the Virgin can be named at no risk. Sometimes the Tío makes pacts with the mine contractors or lessors: he sells them riches in exchange for their souls. It is he who has winked his eye at the peasants so they will abandon their crops and bury themselves forever in the shaft.

Gathered around his great clay image, the miners drink and talk. This is the *ch'alla.* They place candles on the Tío upside down, and offer him cigarettes, beer, and *chica.* The Tío finishes the cigarettes and empties the glasses. At his feet, the miners sprinkle a few drops of brandy, and this is how drink is offered to the earth goddess.

The miners ask the Devil to make the mine flourish.

"Tío, help us. Don't let us die."

The *ch'alla* functions as a political university. The dictators have forbidden it. These men meet around the Tío, in the mine's secret crannies, and talk about their problems and how to change things. They feel protected, they give each other hope and courage. They don't kneel before the Devil. When they leave, they drape colored streamers around his neck.

– 3 –

Women can't enter the mine. An old myth says they bring bad luck.

The old myth has saved them from the early death the mine reserves for its male workers.

Street War, Soul War

Each of my two halves could not exist without the other. Can you love the out-of-doors without hating jails? Live without dying, be born without killing?

Inside my chest—a bull ring—liberty and fear do battle.

The System

Whoever is against it, the machine teaches, is an enemy of the nation. Whoever denounces injustice commits treason against the country.

I am the country, says the machine. This concentration camp is the country: this garbage heap, this immense wasteland empty of men.

Whoever thinks that the country is a house which belongs to everyone shall be the child of no one.

They Buried Him Alive in a Hole

It must be a nerve, tenderness. A nerve that breaks and can't be mended. I've known few people who have survived the tests of pain and violence—a rare feat—with their capacity for tenderness intact.

Raúl Sendic was one of those people.[4]

I wonder, now, what will have remained of him.

I remember him with his baby's smile in that rough, clay face, asking me between his teeth,

"Do you have a razor blade?"

Raúl had just bought a suit, in the store owned by the Turk who sold used clothes, in the Ciudad Vieja, and he felt quite elegant inside that brown serge bag with matching stripes. But the suit didn't have a small pocket in the trousers, so necessary for change. So he made the pocket with a razor blade and some safety pins.

I was fourteen and an illustrator at *El Sol*, the socialist weekly. They had given me a table, in the party headquarters, and there I had a razor blade, drawing ink, tempera paint, and brushes. Every week I had to produce a political cartoon. Raúl thought up the best jokes and his eyes sparkled when he drew near to give them to me.

Sometimes we left the Socialist Youth meetings together.

We lived near one another. He got off at Duilio Street and I stayed on for a few more blocks. Raúl slept on his balcony. He couldn't stand to have a roof over him.

Years later I sometimes asked myself how Raúl had kept himself from going mad during that long time he spent locked up in holes. From barracks to barracks they kept him deep in the earth, with a cover over the top of the hole, and his water and bread were lowered by rope, so he could never see the sun or talk to anyone.

I can't imagine him in this darkness. I see Raúl out-of-doors, in the countryside, seated on a cow's skull—which became his law office's sole chair. The sugarcane workers, who called him "El Justiciero" [the bringer of justice] heard from his lips and understood, for the first time, words like "rights," "union," "agrarian reform."

I close my eyes and again see Raúl in front of a campfire, on the banks of the Río Uruguay. He lifts a live coal to my lips because, bungler that I am, I have let my corn husk cigarette go out again.

Buenos Aires, July 1975: The Men Who Cross the River

Today I discover that once a month, the day the magazine comes out, a group of men cross the Río Uruguay to read it.

There are about twenty of them. The group leader is a professor of about sixty who has spent a long time in prison.

In the morning they leave Paysandú and cross over to Argentine soil. They all chip in and buy an issue of *Crisis* and then go to a cafe. One of them reads aloud, page by page. They all listen and discuss the material. The reading lasts all day. When it ends, they leave the magazine at the cafe as a present for the owner, and return to my country, where it is banned.

"Even if it were just for this," I think, "it would be worthwhile."

This Afternoon I Broke "Porky" and Threw the Pieces Away

She had been everywhere with me. At my side, she had put up with bad weather, physical abuse, and falls. She had lost her wire spiral and her pages had come loose. Just a few strips of her maroon-colored covers were left. "Porky," once an elegant French address book, had been reduced to a heap of pages and scraps held together with a rubber band, frayed, tattered, and full of ink and dirt stains.

It was a difficult decision. I loved that fat shambles. Every time I asked it for an address or phone number it exploded in my hands.

No computer could have dealt with her. "Porky" was in no danger from spies or police. I could find what I needed in her effortlessly; I knew how to decipher her stain by stain and piece by piece.

Between A and Z, "Porky" contained ten years of my life.

I had never copied her over into another book. Laziness, I said—but it was fear.

Today I killed her.

A few names truly hurt me. Most I didn't even recognize. The book was full of people who were dead, and also of those who were alive but had ceased to mean anything to me.

I confirmed that during these years the person who had died and been born several times was I.

My First Death Was Like This

– 1 –

I spent my nights sitting in bed, filling up ashtrays.

Sylvia, innocent one, slept soundly. I hated her at daybreak. I woke her, shook her by the arms, I wanted to tell her, "These are the questions that keep me from sleeping." I wanted to tell her, "I feel alone; me, the hunter, dog that barks at the moon," but I don't know what came out of my mouth instead of words. I think I babbled nonsense, like, "purity, sacred, guilt, hunger for magic." I became convinced I had been born in the wrong century or on the wrong planet.

A few years ago I had lost God. The mirror had broken on me. God had the characteristics I attributed to him and said the words I hoped he would. While I was young, I kept safe from doubt and death. Then I had lost God and didn't recognize myself in others.

Political activism didn't help me, although more than once, coated from head to toe with poster glue, I felt happily weary or a sense of combat which was worthwhile. Around me existed a quiet, tamed world, in which each citizen represented his character (some had a complete cast) and Pavlov's little dogs salivated punctually.

Several times I tried to write. Instinct told me this could be the way to get rid of the beast that had grown inside me. I wrote a word, a sentence sometimes, and then I would scratch it out. After some weeks or months the page was completely scratched up, and it quietly rested in its place on the table, saying nothing.

– 2 –

I wanted to cry. I cried. I had just turned nineteen and preferred to think I cried because of the smoke made by the things I was burning. I built a good-sized fire out of papers, photos, and drawings, so nothing would remain of me. Afterward I went out to a number of pharmacies to buy enough sleeping pills to kill a horse.

I had chosen the hotel. While I walked down Río Branco Street, I felt I had been dead hours or years ago; I was empty of curiosity or of desire, and all I needed was to go through the motions. Nevertheless, when I arrived at San José Street and a car bore down on me, my body, which was still alive, gave a gigantic jump to the curb.

The last thing I remember about my first life is a ray of light from under the closed door as I sank into a serene night which was to never end.

– 3 –

I woke up, after several days of coma, in the prisoners' ward at the Maciel hospital. To me it was a Calcutta marketplace. I saw half-naked men, in turbans, selling knick-knacks. They were so skinny their bones stuck out. They were squatting. Others made snakes dance with flutes.

When I left Calcutta I had no dirt or shadows inside me. My outsides were destroyed, due to the acid in the urine and shit my body had kept churning out, by itself, while I slept my death in the hotel. My body never forgave me. I still have the scars: the onion skin that now prevents me from riding bareback as I like to, because it breaks and bleeds, and on my legs the scars of the wounds that reached my bones. I see them every morning when I get up and pull on my socks.

But this was the least of my worries during those days at the hospital. My eyes had been washed. I saw the world for the first time and wanted to devour it. Every day after that would be a gift.

Now and then I forget, and I give this second life over to sadness. I let myself be expelled from Paradise, every now and again, by that punishing God who never finishes leaving you entirely.

– 4 –

Then I could write and I began to sign my articles and books with my second surname, Galeano.

Until recently I thought I had made this decision due to the phonetic difficulties in Spanish of my paternal name. In the end, this is why I Latinized it: I signed Gius, instead of Hughes, the illustrations which, from a very early age, I published in *El Sol.*

And now, the other night, I realized that calling myself Eduardo Galeano was, from 1959 on, a way of saying: I'm another person, I've just been born, I've been born anew.

In the End, It's All a Question of History

Several centuries before Christ, the Etruscans buried their dead between walls that sang to the joy of life.

In 1966 Graciela and I went into these Etruscan tombs and saw the paintings. There were lovers enjoying one another in all positions, people eating and drinking, scenes of music and celebration.

I had been trained for pain by Catholicism, and my eyes popped out at this cemetery which was a joy.

And of Courage

One night, ages ago, in a small cafe in the Montevideo port, I was drinking all night with a whore friend, and she told me,

"You know something? When I'm in bed with a man, I never look at his eyes. I work with closed eyes. Because if I look at them I go blind, did you know that?"

But You Must Know How to Choose

How many times have we confused bravery with the death wish?

Hysteria is not history, nor a revolutionary someone who loves death.

Death, which had me in her grip a few times and let me go, often calls me still and I tell her to go to hell.

My Second Death Was Like This

— 1 —

I got up, stumbled around, and lit the only lamp in the room. The clock said 8:30 p.m. I opened both sides of the door which let out to a wooden porch overlooking the beach. The full moon excited the dogs. I couldn't sleep, but it wasn't because of the dogs.

Standing made me dizzy. I lay down, folded over the pillow, and tried to read. The bed was boiling. A hot breeze blew the leaves of an almond tree in at my feet.

This had been an important day for me. As I had left the hospital they had given me a certificate of resurrection.

I took a few steps, dizzily, and turned on the shower. I looked at the mirror and saw a heap of bones with sunken eyes.

I felt miserable. My knees were like jelly. My chin shook, my teeth chattered. I rallied all my remaining strength and with both hands squeezed my chin. I wanted to stop that constant chattering. I was unsuccessful.

I sat on the bed with a towel on my knees. The water bounced hard against the cement floor of the bathroom. I sat for some time, thinking nothing and staring at my toes. Rivulets of sweat slithered down my bare body. I wiped off the perspiration and slowly slipped on my pants and shirt.

The shower was still on. I realized I hadn't used it. Getting undressed was too much effort. I turned the shower off and left.

Barefoot, I walked beneath the almond trees of Macuto.

– 2 –

Caracas was a gigantic supermarket. Only cars could live there without rotting away their souls or poisoning their lungs. So I had rented a room in this little hotel on the coast, facing the sea. It wasn't far away. Every day I commuted through the mountains.

It was a good place. The air was always clean and the sun came into the room early and then you could have a good swim before beginning the day. On the coast there was a string of cafes and restaurants, with little tables set under the trees, by the edge of the beach. There were lots of pigeons. It was there I learned for the first time that when the female pigeon touches beaks with the male, she doesn't do it to kiss, but to feed him the milk that springs from her crop.

– 3 –

They had let me go at dusk, truce time.

Alejandro Moldofi, the doctor, had patted my back and said,

"I release you."

And he had said,

"You have had two bouts of malaria in one month. Take care of yourself. You should eat lots of lentils. Here are your pills: quinine, iron."

Now I knew that a mosquito can be worse than a snake and I also knew that I would be haunted to the end of my days, by fear that the fire and ice of that fever would return. In the jungle they call it the cheapie, because it kills you in one day and you don't have to spend your money on medicine.

We had been prisoners of the rain, Daniel Pacheco, Arnaldo Mendoza, and I, in the diamond mines of the Guaniamo jungle. The disaster had been worth it. A man went to bed a millionaire in that place and in the morning he was dead or didn't have a penny to buy a cracker with. Black Barrabás had been the founder of the miners' race. He had discovered a diamond the size of a pigeon's egg and had then had all his teeth pulled out and replacements of pure gold made. He ended his days in a remote mine near the border, buying his breakfasts on credit.

In the camps the miners slept in hammocks strung between the trees. Each hammock was a house, but Ballantine whiskey and French cognac were consumed. A cup of coffee cost ten times more than in Caracas and during those days we found ourselves without a cent. Nena saved us. She came from La Guayra. She was nineteen and in one night of lovemaking earned more than I did each month. When I looked at her legs I thought, "It's fair." Nena gave us beer and food, and finally we managed to get on a small plane that flew us out of the jungle The mosquitoes had devoured us and all three of us carried malaria in our blood. I got both types: the benign and, then, the bad type.

My head felt like an open wound when I reached the hospital. The fever dug into it with knives, lit fire to it. I thought I would die and didn't expect anyone to appear in the middle of my delirium and open their arms to save me from the burning and the knife stabs of the fever; the pain was such that there was no room in me for anything but pain, and I simply wanted to die because death hurt less.

But it was nice to wake up the next morning. The fever had dropped. I blinked, looked around at my neighbors' beds, rubbed my eyes. I was surrounded by faces upon which leishmaniasis had wreaked havoc. Leprosy had eaten their ears, lips, noses; their bones and gums stood out starkly.

I remained there quite awhile. I think I was the only case of malaria. The lepers, of peasant stock, didn't speak. I shared with them the apples my friends brought me. They had a radio. We listened to love songs.

The quinine, a dosage fit for a horse that they stuck in my veins, had saved me. Little by little, I recovered. When I saw my black urine, my dead blood, I was frightened, and still more frightened when the fever returned. I squeezed the doctor's arm and asked him to not let me die, because I didn't want to die anymore, and he laughed and told me to get serious.

– 4 –

Time in the hospital was like a long trip. I was in a train, crossing the world, and out of the night mist cities and lights emerged, faces of loved ones: I bid them good-bye.

I saw the sea and the port of Montevideo and the cooking fires of Paysandú, the corners and the plains where I had been a child and happy. I saw a colt galloping. I saw the mud huts and the ghost towns. Little birds on the back of a cow lying down. The remains of a ruined ranch. I saw myself entering the w d-covered chapel. I stuck the huge key in the hole and the door creaked and groaned. Larks and lapwings chirped outside.

Light shone through the stained glass windows and bathed my face in red light while I made my way through the weeds and reached the altar and chatted with God and lost him.

I saw my brother waking me up under the trees, shaking me, the morning of the third day of our horseback trip in the open country. He woke me and asked, "Have you ever been with a woman?" And I stretched awake and lied to him.

I saw seas and ports. Suburban bars, smoke-filled, smelling of hot food. Prisons. Faraway regions. Little towns lost in the mountains. Campfires. I saw looks, wombs, flashes: women loved under the pounding rain or by the sea or on trains, women pinned against a tree on a street at midnight, embraces of beetles rolling down sand dunes. I saw my children and the friends I never again heard about.

I had spent my entire life saying good-bye. All my life saying good-bye. What was the matter with me? After so many good-byes, what had I left? And inside me, what had been left? I was thirty years old, but between my memory and the desire to go on a great deal of pain and much fear had accumulated. I had been many people. How many identity cards did I possess?

Again I had been on the verge of sinking. I had been saved from dying a death not of my choosing and far from my people, and that joy was more intense than any panic or wounds. It would not have been fair to have died, I thought. This little boat has not yet reached port. But what if there was no port for this little boat to reach? Maybe it was sailing for sheer pleasure or pushed on a mad search for that sea or that luminous sky which I had lost or invented.

To have died now would have been a mistake. I wanted to give everything before death came, empty myself, so that old bitch couldn't find anything to take with her. I still had a lot of kick left in me! Yes. It was that which remained after the good-byes: lots of kick and desire to sail on and world-hunger.

– 5 –

My friends brought me back from the hospital in a car. We reached Macuto just before the sun went down. We sat at a cafe and ordered beer.

Other sunsets emerged from the light of this one. When I was small I had gone fishing, not to fish, which really didn't interest me because I was sorry for the fish, but for the delight of being there on the pier watching the sea slowly eat up the sun. I now felt that same thing in my chest. I felt that one essential thing in me hadn't changed, in spite of everything.

I laughed with my friends. They offered me crutches, told me that malaria had given me St. Vitus' Dance, suggested I begin filing for retirement.

At nightfall they went back to Caracas. I returned to my room to lie down. I tried to sleep but couldn't.

– 6 –

Later I got up and walked. I felt the sand under my bare feet and tree leaves touching my face. I had left the hospital as limp as a rag, but I had left alive and I didn't give a damn about my shaking chin and the laziness of my legs. I pinched myself and laughed. I had neither doubts nor fears. The entire planet was my promised land.

I thought I knew some good stories to tell other people, and I discovered, or confirmed, that I had to write. I had often been convinced that this solitary trade wasn't worthwhile if you compared it, for example, to political activism or adventure. I had written and published a lot, but I hadn't had the guts to dig down inside and open up and give of myself. Writing was dangerous, like making love the way you should.

That night I realized I was a hunter of words. This is what I had been born for. This was going to be my way of being with others after I was dead and this way the people and the things I had loved wouldn't die.

To write I had to get my feet wet. I knew. Challenge myself, provoke myself, tell myself, "You can't do it, I bet you can't." And I also knew that in order for the words to come I had to close my eyes and think intensely about a woman.

– 7 –

Then I got hungry and I dropped into the Chinese restaurant in Macuto. I sat by the door, to catch the fresh sea breeze.

At the back of the restaurant was a girl eating by herself. I saw her profile, and didn't pay much attention. Anyway, I'm shortsighted and didn't have my glasses.

I can't remember what I ate. Egg rolls, I suppose, and soup and stir-fried chicken or something like that. I had beer, which is always preferable to bad wine. I drank the beer the way I like to, with the cold froth on my lips and the golden liquid flowing through the froth bit by bit against my teeth.

As I ate I forgot the trembling of my chin. My hand was steady as it raised the fork to my mouth.

I looked up. The pale girl approached, with slow steps, from the back.

She picked up a little paper dart from the floor and ripped it into pieces. I looked at her, she looked at me.

"I sent you a message," she said.

I swallowed and smiled apologetically.

"Sit down," I invited. "I didn't notice."

I asked her what the message had said.

"I don't know," she replied.

"Sit down," I repeated, and moved out the chair for her.

She shook her head, hesitated. At last she sat down. She looked at the floor uncomfortably.

I wanted to continue eating, but it was difficult.

"It looks like you don't get much sun," I said.

She shrugged her shoulders.

The rest of the meal got cold in the plate.

She reached out, looking for a cigarette. I caught sight of the scars on her wrist.

I lit the cigarette. She coughed.

"They're strong," she said.

She examined the package, turning it over in her hand.

"They're not from here," she said.

The light licked her face. She was beautiful, despite her pallor and thinness. She stared at me and I wanted her to smile and didn't know how to make her.

"So you know why I threw the paper?" she asked, and said, "Because you look like a madman."

In the background I think there was some doleful Chinese music, played quite low. A woman's voice, if I'm not mistaken, which broke off in the middle of every wail.

"I never get sun," she said. "I spend all day locked up in my room."

"And what do you do, locked up there?"

"I wait," she said.

– 8 –

They finally switched off the lights—a very un-Chinese way of kicking us out—and we walked a few paces to the sand. We sat down.

I looked up at the sky of that country. It was different from our sky. I began to hunt for stars. To my surprise I discovered the Southern Cross on the horizon. The pale girl told me that the Southern Cross could be seen in May.

She spoke as if she had been silent for years. She talked and chewed her nails. Her nails were all bitten off.

My knees were weak and my eyes heavy; my chin had begun to shake again. But I felt good there.

I don't know why I told her she was lovely but thin, and she defended herself. She raised her skirt so I could feel her leg.

Then we walked a few blocks under the trees. She pointed vaguely toward some red-tiled houses in a narrow little street leading down to the beach.

"I live there," she said.

I also liked her slightly hoarse voice.

She paused, rested her back against a wall.

It was hot. There were mosquitoes in the lamplight.

"Forgive me for talking so much," she said.

She bit her lips. A little drop of blood rolled down toward her chin.

— 9 —

I enjoyed watching her take her clothes off in the blue moonlight. She had been right to insist her thinness was illusory.

I think I never did it worse. It was an accomplishment to move an arm. I withdrew from her and passed out.

She shook me awake.

"What's that?"

I turned over, rubbed my eyes.

On one side of the open door, two golden eyes glimmered, awesome in the dark.

"I don't know," I said. "A cat."

I was slipping back to sleep again when she squeezed my arm.

"Look," she said.

"What?"

"It's still there."

The eyes didn't blink or move.

Then I couldn't sleep either.

I switched on the light and couldn't see a cat or anything. I switched it off and turned my face to the wall. But I felt the shot of electricity on my neck.

The pale girl got up and drew near.

"Leave it alone," I said.

I saw her bend over, I guessed the murmurings that the sound of the sea drowned out. Her body came between the golden eyes and me.

And suddenly she screamed.

– 10 –

I switched on the bed lamp. She was looking at her hand, stupefied. I saw the teeth marks.

"That cat had rabies," she said, and she began to cry.

I had to force my throat to speak. I think I was sincere. I said that dogs transmit rabies, cats don't. Sleep began to overpower me. The girl's hand began to swell.

"Yes," she insisted, "it had. That cat had rabies."

"You don't care if I die," she cried.

She decided to go out and ask. When I stood up, the world did a somersault. I got dressed, I don't know how, and dizzily descended the stairs with her.

We found a sailor sleeping against the stone beach wall. He replied with neither haste nor anger, as he took his first few puffs of a cigarette. In order to find out, the cat had to be chased and caught.

There we were, the three of us, stooping over and calling cats in the dark. We had just one flashlight. Cats of all shapes and colors appeared. We would meow and they would answer, take a look, slip along the cornices and flee.

Every few yards I would sit down on the ground and rally my strength for the next few steps. I wasn't panting because I didn't have enough breath for that. Nor did I blink. Had I closed my eyes once I would have fallen asleep.

– 11 –

Her hand had turned purple. By now her arm was paralyzed, but she didn't complain. She had to go to the hospital. She wanted to go alone. My body had gone on strike. I gave the orders but it didn't move. "Comrade body," I begged. "You can't let me down."

To get to the hospital we had to get to the highway and hope that Divine Providence would send us a taxi. The highway was at the other side of a long, steep hill.

In the hospital they gave her serum. The pale girl came out with her hand bandaged. She said, dryly, that she had to go to Caracas, to the anti-rabies institute, every day for the next two weeks, to get shots. The first injection was at eight in the morning. I promised to go with her. She said nothing.

When we got back, the early morning mist was rising on the horizon. In the first rays of light a fishing boat appeared off the beach.

I climbed up the steps like a sleepwalker and buried myself in bed. I think I managed to set the alarm at the right place, but I didn't wind it.

It was 4:00 p.m. when I woke up.

– 12 –

I searched for her.

House by house, I looked for her on the block where she had said she lived. I didn't know her name. I offered what I could: the face, the pallor of her skin, the clothes, her neckscarf, her sandals. Nobody had seen her. Nobody had heard of her.

I went down by the shore. I walked, asked, persisted.

I had to go to Caracas. It was late when I got back.

The waiter at the Chinese restaurant was sweeping the floor with sawdust. He leaned on the broom, smiled and nodded, but said nothing.

The Sun Extinguished the Colors and Shapes of Things

Five years later I returned to Macuto.

The Alemania Hotel was not the same. I found the wicker armchairs on the porch falling apart, the mosquito netting on the doors torn, the floors and walls more battered and the faces of the old couple who spent their days in the shade of the entranceway more opaque.

Outside there was, as usual, sun and pigeons and people.

My room was empty. I slept in the same bed, worn by other bodies, and woke up early.

I couldn't find the swimsuit I had left drying on the porch. It could have been a thief, who had found no way in and had decided it wasn't worth it, or the wind, which was nonexistent. Maybe Macuto had to grab something away from me and keep it.

I spent the day walking along the coast.

It was very hot. The light shimmered, boiled, you stared at a point in the air and a white fire would start. Luis Britto is right in saying that light in the tropics is an army of ants that devours what it touches.[5] Macuto light, daggers from the eyes of God: the painter Reverón, who had built his stone house there, went mad pursuing it and died without catching it.

But I Prefer the Radiance of People

– 1 –

"Traitor," I said. I showed him the clipping from a Cuban paper. There he was, dressed as a pitcher, playing baseball. I remember that he laughed, we laughed. I don't know whether or not he answered me. The conversation jumped, like a ping-pong ball, from one subject to the next.

"I don't want every Cuban to wish he were a Rockefeller," he said.

Socialism had meaning to the extent that it purified people, moved them beyond egoism, saved them from competition and greed.

He told me that when he was president of the central bank he had signed the bills with the word "Che" to poke fun, and he told me that money, that shit-awful fetish, should be ugly.

Che Guevara gave himself away, like everyone does, through his eyes. I remember that clean, morning-fresh look: the look of people who believe.

– 2 –

Chatting with him, you couldn't forget that this man had come to Cuba after a long pilgrimage throughout Latin America. He had been in the whirlwind of the Bolivian revolution and in the death throes of the Guatemalan revolution—and not as a tourist. He had loaded bananas in Central America and taken snapshots in Mexican plazas to earn his living, and he had risked his life by throwing himself into the "Granma" adventure.

He was not a man to sit behind a desk. That feline tension so noticeable when I interviewed him in mid-1964 had to explode sooner or later.

His was the unusual case of someone who abandons a revolution which he and a handful of crazy people had already made, to throw himself into beginning another one. He lived not for triumph, but for struggle—the ever necessary struggle for human dignity.

– 3 –

Three years later, my eyes were glued to the front page of the papers. The agency photos showed his motionless body from all angles. General Barrientos' dictatorship displayed its great trophy to the world.

For a long time I looked at his smile—ironic and tender at the same time—and bits of that 1964 dialogue came to my mind. Definitions of the world ("Some people possess the truth, but the matter of life is possessed by others"), of revolution ("Cuba will never be a showcase of socialism, but rather a living example"), and of himself ("I have been mistaken often, but I believe …").

I thought, "He has failed. He is dead." And I thought, "He will never fail. He will never die," and with my eyes fixed on the face of that Jesus Christ of the Río de la Plata I longed to congratulate him.

Buenos Aires, October 1975: The Daily Life of the Machine

– 1 –

Orlando Rojas is a Paraguayan, but he has lived in Montevideo for years.

He tells me the police burst into his house and took his books. All of them—the books on politics and the art books and the history books and those about wildlife. A young plainclothesman in the group had grown livid and shrill when he spied some titles, like an inquisitioner confronted with witches.

An officer rebuked Orlando.

"You yell a lot, but there are ten of you."

"There are ten. Now there are ten," said the Paraguayan, who speaks very slowly, "But when we are eleven …"

They took him away too. They locked him up and then let him go. A week later they locked him up again.

"The declaration got lost."

They mistreated him and expelled him from Uruguay. In Buenos Aires the police were waiting for him. They took away his identification papers.

"I was lucky," Orlando says.

"Get out," I tell him. "They're going to kill you."

– 2 –

I meet Ana Basualdo. She was lucky too.

They blindfolded her and yanked her out of her house in Buenos Aires. She doesn't know where she went. They tied up her hands and legs. A nylon cord was tied around her neck. They hit and kicked her while they asked her about an article she had published.

"This is a Holy War. We have tried and condemned you. Now you'll be shot."

At daybreak they made her get out of the car. They pushed her against a tree. Her face was against the tree and she was blindfolded, but she felt several men get in line and kneel. She heard the click of their guns. A drop of sweat rolled down her neck. Then came the explosion.

Afterward Ana discovered she was alive. She touched herself—she was intact. She heard the sound of cars driving off.

She managed to untie herself and pull off the blindfold. It was raining and the sky was very dark. Dogs were barking someplace. She was surrounded by tall, old trees.

"A morning made to die in," she thought.

Buenos Aires, October 1975: She Never Faded, Though She Knew She Was Lost

– I –

Nine-thirty at night. The porter must have shut down the elevator by now. A window slams shut someplace. Far away, nearby, televisions and motorcycles can be heard. Dog barks, human voices: someone teases, someone protests. Supper is announced, it'll get cold; the smells of frying and of grilled beef penetrate, through the skylight, the air thick with cigarette smoke.

I think about Elda. She is already in the hospital. They have drugged her so she won't suffer or know she is suffering. The doctors fold their arms: there is nothing they can do. I ought to go to the hospital. It's difficult.

The last time Elda didn't say, "When I come out of this will you take me to your house? I feel like Chinese food and wine."

For several days now Elda has not said, "When I come out of this" or "When I'm cured."

Before, she asked for or promised trips to the movies or the beach or Brazil, but now she can't speak and she doesn't say this or anything.

I met her the day Villar Araujo disappeared. Her eyes amazed me—so large and full of lashes and born of pain.

After that we kept on seeing one another.

"Where did you get so much sweetness?"

"When I was small they gave me lots of beets. In Chivilcoy. Know where that is?"

We got together at the "Tolón" or the "Ramos."

– 2 –

The disease had bitten her lungs when she was sixteen. She had been fighting for eight years and she seemed undefeated, but her body had been fiercely punished by the cobalt and the operations and the doctors' mistakes. She said little or nothing about her curse. She had come to an understanding with it and she didn't lie to herself: she kept her medical history in the closet.

When I saw her at her home, before they sent her to the hospital, she could no longer speak because her chest jumped, crazily, with each word. She sipped water and waved her hand to ask for the oxygen mask. Around the bedside were relatives and friends I didn't know. Elda was very pale, her forehead was damp, her head rested on a pillow, and her hair was parted in the front. It was sunny outdoors, and the afternoon light filtered through the curtains. The blue nightgown looked quite good on her, and I told her so. She smiled, sadly, and I drew nearer and saw the first signs of death on her face. Her nose had become more pointed, the skin a bit tight against her gums. Her gaze, listless, was lost in space; a brief spark would light her eyes when she warded away enemies or clouds or flies with her left hand. I kissed her. Her lips were cold.

– 3 –

Once she had told me a dream which pursued her since childhood. The subway train jumped off the tracks and kept moving, crushing the people on the platform. She was there and the train was almost on top of her. She managed to escape, running, and scrambled up the steps. She walked out into the fresh air, happy to have been saved. Then she suddenly remembered she had left something underground. It was necessary to go back into the subway.

– 4 –

I reach the hospital. It is swarming with people. Some cry. I ask for Elda. They open a door so I can go in and see her. She has on her blue nightgown, but the color of her skin has changed and it is all pricked up by needles. She has a tube in her mouth. From her mouth flows a tiny stream of blood.

Her body shakes in violent convulsions, despite the bombardment of sleeping pills and tranquilizers.

I think that God doesn't have the right to do something like this. Then I don't think a damned thing. I walk down the step, sleepwalking and stumbling. I hear the voice of Elda's best friend, who calls me by name. We stand for a long time, face to face, silent, looking at one another. People walk in and out of the hospital door.

And she says,

"That Sunday. Do you remember?"

A century has not gone by. Just ten days, a few weeks. Elda couldn't get out of bed anymore. Little by little her lungs were dying. She no longer breathed—she gasped. She asked me to take her out of there. It was crazy, but no one objected. They dressed her, they combed her hair. We just made it to a taxi. We took short steps, resting every yard or yard and a half. She was suffocating; I held her arm so she wouldn't fall. I suggested a play or a movie. She wanted to come home with me. That Sunday night Elda had three lungs. At dawn she winked at me and could say, smiling, "I made a deal with the Devil."

And now her best friend says to me,

"I want to tell you what she said when she returned. When she returned home she told me, 'Now it doesn't matter if I die.'"

A Girl Navigates Singing in the Crowd

In the subway station the crowd makes way for the girl who sings.

She walks swaying sweetly.

A small basket hangs from her guitar, for the money to be tossed in.

The girl has a clown face and while she walks and sings she winks at the children.

She sings almost secret melodies in the commotion of the station.

I Was Made of Clay, But Also of Time

Ever since I was a little boy I knew that memories didn't exist in Heaven. Adam and Eve didn't have a past.

Can you live each day as if it were the first?

So the Grand Avenues Can Be Opened[6]

– 1 –

I recognized neither the voice nor the name. She said she had met me in 1971, in the "Sportman" cafe in Montevideo, on the eve of her departure for Chile. I had given her a short letter of introduction for Salvador Allende. "Remember?"

"Now I want to see you. I must see you," she said.

And she said she was bringing me a message from him.

I hung up the phone and stared at the closed door. Six months ago Allende had been killed, mowed down by bullets.

I couldn't keep on working.

– 2 –

In the winter of 1963 Allende had taken me to the south. With him I saw snow for the first time. We talked and drank a lot, during the long Punta Arenas nights, while the snow fell on the other side of the windows. He came with me while I bought long underwear. *Matapasiones* [passion-killers] they call them in those parts.

The following year Allende was a candidate for the presidency of Chile. Crossing the coastal mountains together, we saw a large sign which proclaimed, "With Frei, poor children will have shoes." Below, someone scribbled, "With Allende, there won't be any more poor children." He liked this, but knew how powerful the machinery of fear could be. He told me about a maid who had hidden her only dress in the home of her employer in case the Left won and came to take it away. Chile was being flooded with dollars and on city walls bearded men yanked children out of their mothers' arms to take them to Moscow.

In the 1964 elections, the popular front was defeated.[7]

Time passed; we saw more of each other.

In Montevideo I accompanied him to political meetings and demonstrations; we went to soccer games, we shared food, liquor, and *milongas.* He was thrilled by the gaiety of the crowds in the stands, by the celebrations of goals and good plays, the uproar of drums and firecrackers, the showers of confetti. He loved the apple pancakes at the old "Morini" and Santa Rosa Cabernet wine made him smack his lips out of pure politeness, for we both knew Chilean wines are much better. He danced with spirit, but in the style of an old-fashioned gentleman, and he bowed to kiss the hands of the girls.

– 3 –

I saw him for the last time shortly before he became president of Chile. We embraced in a street in Valparaíso, surrounded by the torches of people who were shouting his name.

That night he took me to Concón and in the early hours of the morning we were left alone in the room. He took out a flask of whiskey. I had been in Bolivia and Cuba. Allende didn't trust the nationalist Bolivian military, though he knew he would need them. He asked about our common friends in Montevideo and Buenos Aires. Later he said he wasn't tired. His eyes drooped shut and he continued to talk and ask questions. I propped the window open a bit to smell and hear the sea. Dawn was on its way. That morning Allende would have a secret meeting, there in the hotel, with top officers in the navy.

A few days later we dined at his home with José Tohá, a nobleman straight from an El Greco painting, and Jorge Timossi.[8] Allende told us that the plan to nationalize the copper mines couldn't get through Congress. He was thinking of holding a big plebiscite. Behind the rallying cry of "copper for Chileans," the Popular Unity was going to break through the constraints of bourgeois institutionality. He talked about this. Then he told us part of the conversation he had had with the top navy officials in Concón that morning while I slept in the next room.

– 4 –

And later he was president. I passed through Chile a few times, but never dared take up his time.

Times of great changes and fervor arrived, and the Right launched its dirty war. Things didn't happen as Allende had expected. Chile recovered its copper, iron, nitrate; the monopolies were nationalized and the agrarian reform began to break the back of the oligarchy. But the owners of power, those who had lost the government, had retained control over the arms and the judicial system, the newspapers and the radios. The functionaries didn't function, the merchants hoarded, the manufacturers sabotaged and the speculators played with the currency. The Left, a parliamentary minority, debated in impotency, and the military acted on its own. Everything was scarce—milk, vegetables, spare parts, cigarettes. And nevertheless, in spite of the lines and the anger, 800,000 workers marched through the streets of Santiago a week before the coup, so that no one would think the government was alone. This multitude was empty-handed.

– 5 –

And now the summer of 1974 was over, the Moneda Palace had been razed six months ago, and this woman was seated before me, in my office at the magazine in Buenos Aires, and she spoke to me about Chile and Allende.

"And he asked for you. 'Where is Eduardo?' " he asked. "'Tell him to come here. Tell him I send for him.' "

"When was this?"

"Three weeks before the coup. I looked for you in Montevideo and couldn't find you—you were away on a trip. One day I called your home and they told me you had moved to Buenos Aires. Later I thought it wasn't worth telling you any more."

Summer of '42

Years ago, in Kiev, they told me why the Dynamo players had deserved a statue.

They told me a wartime story.

Ukrania was occupied by the Nazis. The Germans organized a soccer match. The national team from its armed forces against Kiev's Dynamo, made up of textile factory workers: the supermen against the starving.

The stadium is full. The fans shrink, silently, when the victorious army makes the first goal of the afternoon; they ignite when Dynamo ties; they explode when the first half ends with Germany losing 2 to 1.

The commander of the occupying forces sends his assistant to the dressing room. The Dynamo players listen to the warning.

"Our team has never been defeated in occupied territories."

And the threat.

"If you win, we'll execute you."

The players return to the field.

A few minutes later, the third goal for Dynamo. The crowd watches the game standing up, with a continuous roar. Fourth goal, the stadium goes wild.

Suddenly, before it is time, the referee ends the game.

They shot them with their uniforms on, by the edge of a ravine.

Stronger Than Any Sorrow or Dictatorship

In Montevideo during the first period of exile Darcy Ribeiro had a parrot that stood on his shoulders and pulled the hairs out of his chest. The parrot slept on the balcony. The winds are strong on the Montevideo coast. One morning the parrot was found drowned in the Trouville pool.

When I found him again, in Río, Darcy didn't have a parrot. But he jumped up to welcome me, his eyes sparkling; he called me, as usual, his "ideological mulatto." He asked about my work and my life and he told me, with no complaints, the story of his wanderings from country to country. He spoke about Brazil; told me a Volkswagen Republic is not essentially different from a Banana Republic, and in a few minutes he gave me a complete analysis of the structural crisis in Argentina and explained the causes of the Chilean tragedy and told me what could be done in Uruguay.

I listened, fascinated, to his audacious theories and brilliant definitions. Darcy has a mind which, like him, is never quiet, and it's worth knowing that lively intelligence even when it makes mistakes or tries to pursue truth with shots of nonsense. For good reason those who make Marxism their catechism and sociologists who specialize in boring others can't stand him.

Darcy took off his shirt and showed me the scar. He had a terrible L-shaped gash that spanned his back.

"Look," he said, laughing. "I'm the remains of a shark."

Darcy had wanted to be operated on in Brazil. The armed forces had given him permission to die in his country. They had been waiting for him; they took him from the airport to the hospital. Darcy hadn't much strength left. With what he had he managed to touch the nurses' bottoms. They removed a lung and he still lives. The government felt cheated.

That night in Río was the eve of his departure for Lima. Darcy laughed constantly but confessed that the idea of never smoking again bothered him.

"It's serious, isn't it? I smoked five packs a day."

"You know what I discovered?" he asked. "That one really does everything for the pleasure of smoking. Why do you go swimming in the sea? Why do you chat with friends? Why do you read? Why do you write? Why do you make love?"

"The pleasure is in the cigarette," he said. "The ceremony is that."

And he laughed.

Last Voice

In a patio in Asunción, Paraguay, don Jover Peralta raised his fist, which was like a dried branch, against the dictator Stroessner.

"We are going to overthrow that illiterate Führer!" he cried with his remaining voice. "With the truth we're going to overthrow those traitors!"

Old Peralta smelled of urine and he was skin and bones when I listened to him curse for hours.

He told me he had written a letter to some students, explaining to them that they had to fight for an America which was one country, owner of its own wealth and free of Yanquis, but he had given the letter to some guy to take to the post office and he had turned out to be a spy.

He spoke to me about Solano López and his noble death and about the War of the Triple Alliance.[9]

"The Buenos Aires oligarchy has done us much harm," he whispered. "It made us unbelieving, suspicious. The Buenos Aires oligarchy has ruined our souls."

"Nitwits!" he yelled, and to hear him you had to cock your ear.

His small body was lying still beneath the leafy tree. Don Jover could only move his lips, but indignation made his hands and feet tremble. He wore neither shoes nor socks on his feet, which were swollen with chilblain. When night came, he fell asleep.

Jover Peralta had written some books and had fought all his life for a free Paraguay.

Later he died.

The Most Difficult Mission of My Life

– I –

I thought,

"You are better than I am. I know you can take it. You're tough. I have to do it, and I ask you to help me."

That fellow had been through two wars in the hills. When they brought him down on a stretcher, passed out, the only heavy things left on his body were his torn up, muddy boots. They tortured him by hanging him from the ceiling, and they hit him in the kidneys because they knew he was sick and urinated blood. He didn't open his mouth. When he could get up, a little later, he walked into the cell of the traitor and smashed his head in.

"May it help me," I thought. "May it help me screw him."

He had joined the struggle at the age of fourteen. Since then he had lived for the revolution and for a woman. I was going to destroy half his faith for him.

"Goddamned mission," I thought.

He made leather handbags in prison. With his earnings he had someone buy her nylon stockings and shoes. He had a thirty kilo trunk full of new clothes he was going to give her when he returned, because she was going to be waiting for him at the train station.

But this woman lived with another man.

The party had decided to tell him she wanted a divorce. The party wanted to be the first to tell him, before the enemy did. The enemy could use the situation to weaken his conscience and to make him feel alone.

– 2 –

"So she lives with someone else," he answered.

"No, it's not that," I said. "But she wants ... If it were to happen. She wants to be free. She has that right. A long time has passed and you don't know how many more years ... She has the right. Don't you think she has the right? She hasn't played games with you."

"So she lives with someone else," he repeated.

He was a man of few words.

"And if she doesn't live with anyone else, why the divorce? And what is this guy like? Hasn't he given her a child yet?"

– 3 –

Some time later he gave me a letter, wrapped in a cigarette, for me to give to his mother. I have always been very indiscreet about letters. It read:

> Mother—
>
> You have been very stupid to be fooled by that tramp. I knew from the start she would end up in this kind of trouble. Tell her not to come crying to me later.
>
> I want you to go get all my things, every last one. Take the medal, the clothes, the shoes. I received the picture of the kids. Get the kids too. She doesn't have any rights now and she better not deny things later.
>
> Tell Negro to go to Santa Rita and on the main road, in front of the hospital, by the bus stop, is Amanda's house—or ask Chino where it is. She has black hair and a bracelet with ceramic flowers that I made for her as a present. He should tell Amanda to get ready for my return some long time from now.
>
> Also tell Clara, Ernesto's cousin, to wait for me. She lives behind the Enramada cemetery, by the big acacia.
>
> Greetings to all, and bless you.

(This took place some years ago, in a place I cannot name.)

Buenos Aires, October 1975: The Violent Light of Glory

Today Bidente came to see me. He told me about his escape from Uruguay and I got up to date on his latest adventures. He told me he'd be visiting his grandson in Dakar soon.

Bidente, thus named because he has two teeth, is forty years old this week. "At forty you can be a saint or a scoundrel. But pure," he warned.

Bidente is an admirable oral narrator. I envy him. He knows how to save himself through fantasy, and can almost always use whatever is offered him. He sits in front of you and transports you.

During World War II he belonged to General Stern's troops, which evacuated Jews through the Warsaw sewers.

The liberation finds him in Paris. There he learns about the mysteries of love. A Japanese woman reveals to him, on long beds, the secret language of fingertips and tongues and she teaches him to discover the universe of moles, pores, and cartilages.

In Paris Bidente is a judo and karate champion. An Arab sheikh contracts him to organize his mercenary army. The war against the republicans is long and hard. Bidente drags himself across the desert with the only soldier to survive. Days and nights sharing thirst and hope: they proceed in silence across the dunes, laugh together, cry together. They can't talk because they don't understand each other. At the end of a terrible crossing, they reach the Mecca. That night, in the Mecca Hilton, a dinner to celebrate. They are bathed, shaved, they wear clean tunics. The Arab toasts and the interpreter translates. The Arab says that he has never seen a man of such courage, and he asks him to be his for the night.

In the Amazon Bidente spends two years with the Bororo Indians. He passes the nine tests of the warrior. The hardest is that of ants on the honey-coated body. The tribe accepts him as a son. He doesn't make love to Indian girls. If he did, he would have to remain there forever: no one can escape from this village. In the surrounding jungle, Bidente has counted, one by one, eight thousand jaguars.

In Manaos an American anthropologist contacts him. They travel by canoe. She is a splendid blond. Bidente rubs turtle grease on her bare back to keep the mosquitoes away. When they finally reach a Xavante village, after a few shipwrecks and ambushes, the chief suggests,

"I'll exchange her for my daughter."

"She isn't my wife," Bidente explains.

"Stupid," the chief says. "Don't you see that you get a better deal that way?"

Bidente goes up and down the river.

Once, in a state of exhaustion, he arrives at an Indian reservation in the Alto Xingu. There he finds a priest who offers him a hammock so he can sleep in the priest's hut. They eat fruit and drink firewater. The priest talks too much. He tells Bidente how he exploits the Indians by taking their valuable handicrafts and giving them little pictures of the Virgin. Bidente gets suspicious. He realizes he has become a dangerous witness. He pretends he is drunk, and lets his head nod sleepily. But he sleeps with his netting fastened tight so the hammock will vibrate with any footsteps. At midnight the priest approaches his hammock on tiptoes and aims his shotgun at him. Bidente jumps up and cuts his head off with a machete.

Bidente goes down river. In the first police station he finds an officer, Seu Zacarias, an old friend. He tells him what has happened. Seu Zacarias walks over to the canoe, grabs the priest's head by the hair and throws it into the river.

"*As piranhas vão fazer o expediente*" ["The piranhas will do what is necessary"], he says, and offers Bidente a cup of coffee.

The next year, in Colombia ...

Rio De Janeiro, October 1975: This Morning He Left His House and Was Never Seen Alive Again

— 1 —

We are in the "Luna"; we drink beer, we eat crabs.

My shoes are white from talcum powder and my friends want to convince me you put the talcum on first.

This afternoon a journalist interviewed me in Galeno de Freitas' home. She taped two or three hours of conversation. Nothing was recorded. The only thing on the tape was a buzz. Zé Fernando proposed an article on the sexual life of bees.

Zé announced a banquet, a huge platter of Brazilian-style bass, next Sunday at his house in Niteroi.

I ask for more crab, and then more, and they say I'm like a school of piranhas.

We laugh about anything that night, in the "Luna," everything is funny; and we fall silent when, at the door, a large-eyed, olive-skinned woman appears, wearing a red bandana around her head, gypsy-like. She allows herself to be seen for an instant, for an instant she is a goddess, and then she vanishes.

– 2 –

We are in the "Luna" when Ary brings the news.

"They've suicided him," he says.

Torres had told him by phone. They had sent the news from São Paulo.

Eric gets up, pale, open-mouthed. I squeeze his arm; he sits down again. I know he had arranged a meeting with Vlado and that Vlado had neither arrived at the meeting place nor called.

"But he wasn't involved in anything," Eric says.

"They killed him for not knowing anything," Galeno says.

"The machine is crazy," I think or say. "They must have blamed the Russian Revolution on him."

Eric says, "I thought this had ended." His head falls into his hands. "I ... " he complains.

"No, Eric," I say.

"You don't understand," he says. "You don't understand anything. You don't understand a damned thing."

The glasses are empty. I order more beer and ask them to fill our plates.

Eric looks at me furiously and goes into the bathroom.

I open the door. I find him with his back against the wall. His face is drawn and his eyes wet; his fists clenched.

"I thought this had ended. I thought all this had ended," he says.

Eric was Vlado's friend and he knows what Vlado had done and all that he was going to do and couldn't.

– 3 –

Not long ago Eric's boy was born. His name is Felipe.

"In twenty years," Eric says, "I'm going to tell him the things that are happening now. I'll talk to him about the friends who are dead and in prison and about how hard life was in our countries, and I want him to look in my eyes and not believe me and tell me I'm lying. The only proof will be that he was here, but he won't remember anything about this. I want him to not be able to believe that this was possible. I want him to say that this time never existed."

– 4 –

Felipe was born at 5:30 a.m. on September 4. Eric phoned his best friend in São Paulo.

"Marta is having a baby. I feel lonely. I feel bad."

The friend promised to be there in half an hour, but fell back asleep and never arrived.

Eric walked out into the street. He bought a newspaper and paid with a 100-cruzeiro bill.

"No," said the newspaper man. "I don't have change."

Eric raised his hand and pointed to the maternity ward.

"See?" he said. "My wife is having a baby in that building. Come have a beer with me. You can treat me with the change."

– 5 –

Felipe is in the crib and Eric tells him things.

"You know I'm very dumb when it comes to gasoline. I ran out of gas again today. You'll have to tell me when we pass a gas station."

He says, "You were born with everything already decided. You have a father who will never slow down and who will never have money. Your father's friends have been screwed. Now we're going to Buenos Aires. Sorry, I'm not being fair. I'm taking you and you can't even object."

And he thinks,

"And if tomorrow he thinks the world has not gone astray? And if he would rather have been a stockbroker's son?"

He picks him up, takes him to the terrace, shows him the plants.

"Look. That's the second jasmine we've had in four years. The first one never flowered. This gave us four. They blossomed when I was away. I was sorry I couldn't have seen them flower. I killed the pests on the jasmine and I was able to see the shoots come up. Now I'll have to wait a year. I had to go, you know. There was nothing else to do. I had to work."

In the country, Eric climbs trees so Felipe can see how it's done.

– 6 –

Vlado Herzog showered, shaved, kissed his wife.[10] She didn't get up to see him to the door.

"There's nothing to be afraid of," he said. "I present myself, I explain everything, and I come home."

The news report that night was prepared under his name. When people were watching the evening news, he was already dead.

The official communiqué stated that he had hanged himself. The authorities did not permit a new autopsy.

Vlado was not buried in the space allotted to suicides.

The public security chief of São Paulo declared, "This is a crude war, a naked war, and it is a war in which we have to use the same techniques as our enemies if we don't want to be defeated. We are going to eat them for lunch before they feast on us for supper."

– 7 –

Do you know what the sunrise in Rio looks like, brother, from the window in your house? A lightness from the sky rises behind the tiled roofs and the hills slowly turn purple. Rain-laden clouds flee. A bird flies near you, like a whip: it is the sign of a new day. The clean air gives you shivers and swells your chest. Your house, my house: the sea is over there, it can't be seen anymore because of those damn new buildings, but I smell it, shellfish smell, war of the waves, and I know that someday she will swallow me and take me away, she, the sea, gluttonous goddess in white.

We go to the "Lamas" to say good-bye. Soon it will be demolished and there will be no place to breathe this mixed aroma of fruit and tobacco and times gone by. As we enter the "Lamas" we pass through mountains of oranges, bananas, pineapples, guayabas, and maracuyas.

Sad and silent, we drink beer, one glass after another. From a table in the back, Canarinho, a regular of the Rio bars, attacks the world.

"I read Nietzsche and you don't know anything," Canarinho attacks.

He is small and thin and alone and very drunk. A whistle from his chest escapes after every sentence. A canary whistle.

"We can't stop talking," he says, and he whistles.

"And we're always going to talk. Do they think they can shut us up? No! No! Cowards!"

Canarinho whistled.

"They're all young. They hate the young!"

And he whistled.

"São Paulo can't stop killing. Can't stop killing."

And he whistled.

The System

A half-million Uruguayans outside their country. A million Paraguayans, half a million Chileans. The boats depart full of young people fleeing from prison, the grave, or hunger. To be alive is a risk; to think, a sin; to eat, a miracle.

But how many people are in exile within the borders of their own country? What statistic records those condemned to resignation and silence? Is not the crime of hope worse than the crime of the people?

The dictatorship is an infamous pattern: a machine that makes you deaf and dumb, incapable of hearing, impotent when you speak and blind to that which you are not allowed to observe.

The first person killed by torture triggered a national scandal in Brazil in 1964. The tenth person to die of torture barely made the papers. Number fifty was accepted as "normal."

The machine teaches you to accept horror as you accept the cold of winter.

Buenos Aires, November 1975: I Like to Feel Free and Stay Here if I Want

— I —

Drops of perspiration slide down and fall, clip, clop, on the papers scattered over the table. This desk is a pigpen. The papers advance, come toward me, close me in. The letters I should answer get mixed up with the articles to be edited and the titles of yet unread manuscripts. I pass my hand over my brow. My hand moves through the mountain of papers, poking, probing. I can't find my handkerchief. My cigarettes turn up instead. I get up to steal some matches. My crotch burns when I walk.

Sticking out among the papers is the letter from Marta, the widow of Rodolfo Gini. It's been a year now since they finished him off. They pulled him out of his house in Huangeulén at daybreak and then threw him on the road five kilometers away, his body riddled with bullets. Since then his wife brings or sends me things he had written and which she keeps finding. I have become friends with this man I never knew. He draws close through the words he left. "Can you love the river and not love the sea?" he wrote. "God doesn't live because he can't die. This is why God doesn't know or love you."

Gini was a professor. He had committed no crime other than teaching his students to look straight at the world.

"I think every night is the last," Marta writes me. "I'm not afraid for myself, but for the children." (On that night she loosened her gag with her teeth and yanked her wrist binds off and yelled and ran in the darkness.) The next day her ten-year-old son looked at the crucifix and asked,

"Mama, when those men came in, was He here? I thought that where He was those kinds of things didn't happen."

— 2 —

Letter from Juan Gelman, from Rome. He was the editor of the magazine [*Crisis*]. Some time ago he became a marked man. He hopped on a plane and escaped by the skin of his teeth.

"For the past three weeks I've had palpitations of the heart," he writes, "and I can't do anything about it. It's not because I feel guilt—stupid Christian guilt—but because I'm far away and, above all, because the gravity of what is going on there comes up against a rubber wall here. Uncontrollable fits of anger and anguish come over me and the final result is these palpitations, which neither leave me nor let me breathe.

"Excuse the solemnity. I haven't let go in a while. It's quite difficult to write to Buenos Aires. I don't know whether it's self-defense or the urge to avoid—not pain itself—but talking about it. I know things are very bad and that gives me nightmares.

"As you can see, it's hard for me when it comes to loving. Most of the time I can manage by just making love. I know this is not sufficient. There are a lot of us around whose capacity to love has been damaged, but you need to have courage to bring it out, flaws and all. I now think this is something you have to learn to do, like so many things in life. We will die learning, if we want to live heedless of death."

I can see Juan now, the morning he dropped a package wrapped in newspaper and tied up with a string on the table. In it were all his clothes and belongings. He said,

"I had to move. I don't know where I'll go. I'm going out to look. Take care of my things."

He turned around with his hand on the doorknob and added,

"But first tell me the story about the hen, because I'm sad."

It was one of Paco Espínola's stories. Juan knew it by heart, but still choked with laughter every time I told it. Paco had restored his family's honor by slitting the throat of a feisty hen which had rejected his advances.

How could I help him now, so far away?

I write him a letter in jest.

Juan says it's hard for him, but he can open up and give of himself. "Like bread to the mouth," he was able to write one woman, "like water to the earth, I hope I'm of some use to you." And he could ask her, "Your feet walk in my feet, your feet. Be in me like wood in the twig." Because Juan, the poet, wanted her body to be the only country where he could be defeated.

– 3 –

My hands sink into my pockets. I stretch my legs. Drowsiness brings on shudders of pleasure and fatigue. I feel the night enveloping the city. It is late. I'm alone.

I shouldn't stay here alone. I know this. But tonight I let myself stay, I hang around, doing nothing or opening the little doors to my imagination or my memory.

Lazy. I'm stuck to the chair. It's the heat, probably, or maybe it's just that I'm stuck.

I hear many people, familiar or invented, whistling to me in my head. Inside me faces and words cross and mix together. They appear, grow, fly. Am I this ear that listens or am I the melody? I am not the eye that sees: I'm the images.

– 4 –

The telephone rings and I jump. I look at my watch. Nine-thirty in the evening. Should I answer or not? I answer. It's the José Rucci Commandos from the Argentine Anticommunist Alliance.

"We're going to kill you, you bastards."

"The schedule for calling in threats, Sir, is from six to eight," I answer.

I hang up and congratulate myself. I'm proud of myself. But I want to stand up and I can't: my legs are limp rags. I try to light a cigarette.

The System

The hooded prisoners recognize one another by their coughs.

Someone is butchered for a month and then they tell what remains of him, "It was a mistake." When he leaves, he has lost his job. All his papers as well.

A professor can be fired for reading or saying something questionable, and he loses his job if they arrest him, even if it is only for an hour and by mistake.

Uruguayans who at public ceremonies sing the verse of their national anthem that says, "Tremble, tyrants!" with particular emphasis can be sentenced for "attacking the morale of the armed forces" to a minimum of eighteen months and a maximum of six years in jail. For scratching "Long Live Liberty" on a wall or tossing a leaflet into the street, people can remain in jail, if they survive the torture, most of their lives. If they don't survive, the death certificate will say they tried to escape, stumbled and fell over a cliff, hanged themselves, or died of asthma. There will be no autopsy.

A new jail is inaugurated each month. It's what the economists call the "Development Plan."

But what about the invisible jails? What official report or denunciation by the opposition lists those who are imprisoned by fear? Fear of losing one's job, of not finding work; fear of talking, of listening, of reading. In the country of silence, the light in your eyes can land you in a concentration camp. It's not necessary to fire a functionary: it's enough to let him know he can be summarily sacked and that no one will give him work in the future. Censorship truly triumphs when each citizen is transformed into the implacable censor of his own acts and words.

The dictatorship turns barracks and police stations, abandoned railroad cars and unused boats into prisons. Does it not turn each person's home into a jail as well?

Buenos Aires, November 1975: He Woke Up in the Mud

He was awakened by the rain, which beat down fiercely somewhere in the delta. The Tigre delta was brown and he thought that they were the rivers of Hell. He stumbled around the islands. Then he entered a cafe and sat next to the fire. They brought him wine and he called a woman over to his table. When he invited her she was blond, but as the hours passed her coloring changed and she became many years older. He squeezed the witch's claws between his hands and told her his brother had died in Montevideo, a stupid death, and that he hadn't been able to go, nor could he now, but that wasn't the worst thing. The worst thing was something else, he said, and she wanted to leave and he didn't let her. The worst was that he couldn't remember when had been the last time they had been together, nor what they had said to one another, nor anything else.

Emilio Casablanca tells me this and doesn't know whether it happened yesterday or a year ago and I can see him now in that bar on Soriano Street, one stormy night, when he arranged a row of red wine bottles against the wall and smashed them one by one with his fist and afterward he couldn't paint for a long time.

We ran into each other by chance, on a corner in Buenos Aires. Now we are going to eat together. Tomorrow we'll go to the fair. We're going to take his little girl, because the sky is full of stars and tomorrow is sure to be a lovely day.

The System

It was the birthday of Karl's father. For once he was allowed to stay up after dinner with the grownups. He sat in a corner, quietly looking at the friends and relatives who drank and chatted. When he got up, Karl bumped against a table and knocked over a glass of white wine.

"Don't worry," said his father.

His mother swept up the broken glass and cleaned the floor with a mop. His father took Karl to his bedroom and said,

"At eleven o'clock, when the guests have gone, I'll hit you."

For more than two hours Karl listened to the voices and counted the minutes from his bed.

At exactly 11:00 his father came in, took off his belt and beat him.

"I do it for your own good, so you will learn," his father said, as usual, when Karl cried, naked, his head buried in his pillow.

Some years ago, in Montevideo, Karl told me this story about his childhood in Germany.

Buenos Aires, December 1975: Communions

I gather firewood, bring water from the river.

"Taste it, maestro. It's done."

"Mmmm."

"You really like it?"

"Fantastic job, brother."

We have found some quite tasty, greaseless sausages. It's worth letting the pork linger in your mouth. And then we dig into the rib roast, cutting it bone by bone on the barbeque rack and eating it bit by bit, as one should. We choke a little, but from laughter.

"The *chinchulines* [small sausages] came out very dry. They're crunchy."

"I pinched them before putting them on. That's the secret."

We let the wine breathe—a couple of bottles of red Carcassone—and we taste it and feel it slip down, warm, thick, into our bellies and veins.

We eat and drink until not one bone is left on the barbeque. Eduardo catches the last bite on the end of his fork. I look at him with hungry dog eyes and think, "He's going to take pity on me," but unperturbed, he gobbles it up.

Later we lie down on the grass, with the sun on our faces and the whole island to ourselves. We smoke. There are no mosquitoes. The breeze whistles through the casuarina trees. Every now and then we hear the sound of oars.

Eaten alone, that barbeque shared with Eduardo Mignogne would have had little or no taste. In a way we make, together, that marvelous taste of the meat and the wine. We eat and drink as if celebrating, with our mouths and at the same time our memories. At any moment either of us could be stopped by a bullet, or could become so lonely he wished this would happen, but none of this is of the slightest importance.

When I wake up from my nap, Eduardo is sitting on the pier, his legs hanging over. The dawning light darts through the waters of the Gambado.

"I had a dream, the other night," he says. "I forgot to tell you. I dreamt that we came here on the passenger boat. We were seated across from each other, in the stern, chatting. No one else was nearby. The other passengers were all together in the seats near the bow, quite far away from us. Just then I looked at them and noticed something strange. They were very still and silent and were all exactly alike. I said, 'Wait a minute,' and walked to the other end. I touched one of the passengers and plop, he fell to the floor. As he landed his plaster head fell off. I yelled, 'Jump out, jump out!' and I jumped too. We swam underwater. When I lifted my head out of the water I saw you. We ducked under again and continued to swim desperately. We were quite far away when the boat blew up. I felt the explosion and looked up again. I saw the smoke and the flames. You were beside me. I hugged you and woke up."

Buenos Aires, December 1975: Communions

Jairo calls me. He arrived from Porto Alegre yesterday, he'll be in Buenos Aires a few days. He invites me to dinner.

We haven't seen each other for five or six years. I'm taken aback. I don't let on. His face is deformed, one eye half closed, and his smile is twisted. His left hand, hook hand, moves little; a glove protects it from the cold night air.

We walk in the downtown area. Jairo's body sways, he pushes me unintentionally. He stops, breathes deeply. He's bothered by pangs of pain in his side. He's nervous. He walks and spits.

I don't ask questions. Sometimes he mentions the accident. "When I had the accident," he says, or "Since the accident."

He tells me about his historical research, the fascinating documents he has discovered in Portugal, the life in the *mocambos* [huts] of Palmares, the insurrections in the city of Salvador; he explains his thesis about slavery as the center of Brazilian history.

We enter a restaurant. The conversation continues. Jairo has studied Paraguay in the era of the Francia dictatorship in depth. We disagree. Neither do we agree about the Montonero *caudillos* in Argentina during the past century.

But that isn't what he wants to talk about. The whole time I sense there is another sound in the background, another melody.

We order more wine.

At last he talks to me about that woman. He tells me of the ardent love and he tells me that one night she found him with another woman. Two weeks later Jairo went to ask for forgiveness. She said nothing. He kissed and caressed her. She asked him,

"Do you want to make love to me?"

And she said,

"If you do, you have to pay me."

And he sat down and looked at her.

"How much do you charge?" he asked.

"Three thousand *cruzeiros*," she said.

He slowly filled in the check. He signed it, blew it dry, and passed it to her.

She put the check away and said,

"Wait for me while I go out to buy cigarettes."

Then he was alone. He lunged against the glass windowpane and jumped. He ended up sprawled on the pavement. Her apartment is on the third floor.

They didn't see one another for some time. When they met, he was on crutches. They embraced, insulting each other.

I order another bottle of wine.

"I'm tired of lying," Jairo says. "Everyone asks me what happened and I say it was a crash. I was in my car on the highway and ... Lately I've even been filling in the details."

Buenos Aires, December 1975: Communions

Luis Sabini, the magazine's production manager, has disappeared.

We are hopeful that he has been imprisoned, but the police deny this. Fico and Aníbal have hunted high and low. It's been over a week and we have no news.

Sometimes, at night after work, Luis would stay and talk to me about his father, who had come to Montevideo from a town in Parma which had one hundred houses and a church.

When Luis was small they made wine in his home in Montevideo. They would crush the grapes with bare feet, and the unfermented wine would reach their thighs. They would all get drunk from the fumes. The moon decided when the decanting in oak barrels would take place.

Every wine had a name. "Kiss Me and See," was the strong red. "Crazy Black," the table wine. "Grugnolino," the red that was so thick a spoon would stick in it.

He Entered the New Year in an Empty Train

Ariel left the home of a Chilean who had just died. He had died far from his own country.

The air would soon be gray, announcing the first day of 1976. Ariel was also far from his country and the coming daybreak in France would be meaningless to him. In Ariel's country it was another time, Chilean time. Around the tables in Chile there were empty chairs and the survivors were raising their wine glasses and just beginning to celebrate the end of a lousy year.

Ariel Dorfman walked, slowly, through the streets of this remote Paris suburb.

He sank into the train station. He listened to the echo of his own footsteps and looked for some other human being in the empty train cars.

He found the only other passenger and sat down in front of him.

Out of his pocket Ariel pulled the novel *The Clown* and started to read.

The train departed and a few moments later the man said,

"I'd like to be a clown," looking at the black window.

Ariel did not look up from his book.

"Must be a sad profession," he said.

"Yes," he said, "but I am sad."

Then they looked at one another.

"I am sad, you are sad," Ariel said.

The man said that together they could make a fine pair of clowns and Ariel asked him where, at which circus.

"At any," said the man. "At any circus in my country."

"And which is your country?"

"Brazil," the man said.

"*Chucha*! Then I can talk to you in Spanish!"

And they flew into a conversation about their lost lands as the train slid toward Paris.

"I am sad," said the man, "because I want us to win, but in my heart I don't think we will."

Then they said good-bye, with raised fists.

Buenos Aires, January 1976: Introduction to Music

– 1 –

Julio is staying at my place. He had to leave Montevideo. They imprisoned him for the seventh time and he had to leave. He's out of money and down in spirits; he can't find work.

Tonight we had veal cutlets and salad, which he fixed, and we drank wine.

Julio lies on the bed and smokes. I'd like to listen to him and help him, but he's silent, he doesn't share his pain. I'm an absurd shadow myself. I don't wake things up when I touch them—they fall from my hands.

I select a record—Italian baroque. I don't know when I bought it or with whom: I don't remember having heard it before.

Albinoni comes at just the right moment.

We celebrate the music, hum along with it; the room suddenly fills up with good news.

– 2 –

One of Paco Espínola's stories comes to mind.

I seem to hear Paco: the low, hoarse, scraping voice, the unlit cigarette hanging from his mouth, sitting in groups around the fire or in the cafe until the early hours. There was a witch doctor on the outskirts of San José, an old black man, illiterate, whom Paco had met as a child. The man received people as he sat under an ombu tree. He wore glasses to examine his patients with the eyes of a doctor and to pretend he was reading the paper.

The whole town loved and respected him. Like any true witch doctor, he knew how to save people with weeds and with mysteries.

One afternoon they brought him a wretchedly sick young woman. She was skin and bones, quite pale; she had lost her appetite, couldn't talk, and didn't even have the strength to walk.

The witch doctor made a sign and the woman's parents and brother drew over to the tree.

He, seated, meditated; they, standing, waited.

"Family," he said, at last.

And he diagnosed.

"The soul of this girl is scattered all over."

And he prescribed,

"Music is needed to gather it all together again."

It Was a Gray, Biting Cold Morning

One dawn in late June 1973 I arrived in Montevideo on the steamship that crosses the river from Buenos Aires.

I was standing at the bow. I had my eyes fixed on the city that slowly drew near in the fog.

My country had been hit by two misfortunes and I didn't know it. Paco Espínola had died and the armed forces had carried out a coup and had dissolved the parties, the unions, and everything else.

I Could Not See Light nor Walk More than Three Paces

Returning from another trip shortly before the coup, I learned that the police had been to my home in Montevideo looking for me.

I presented myself to the police alone. I felt afraid as I entered. The door snapped shut behind my back, like a trap. The fear lasted for an hour. Then it left my body. What could happen, worse than death? It wouldn't be the first visit.

I stood in the yard, my face to the wall. The floor above was a torture chamber. Prisoners passed behind me. They were dragged through the yard. Some returned beaten to a pulp; they were thrown onto the ground. At midnight the siren sounded. I heard the commotion, the insults, the excitement of the pack of hounds as it lunged off to the manhunt. The police returned at dawn.

A few days later they put me in a car. They moved me and locked me in a cell.

I scratched my name on the wall.

At night I heard screams.

I began to feel the need to talk to someone. I made friends with a little mouse. I didn't know whether I would be locked up for days or years, and before long one loses count. It was days. I've always been lucky.

The night they let me out I heard murmurings and distant voices and sounds of metal clanking while I walked through corridors, a guard at either side. Then the prisoners began to whistle, softly, as if blowing on the walls. The whistling grew louder and louder until one voice, every voice as one, broke into song. The song shook the walls.

I walked home. It was a warm, serene night. Autumn was arriving in Montevideo. I learned that the week before Picasso had died.

A short time passed and my exile began.

Buenos Aires, January 1976: Reencounter

– 1 –

Cristina tells me about her exorcism rites. She has locked herself up alone in her house, for days and nights, and has called to the living and to the dead and to the forgotten. She has settled accounts, she tells me, with all of them. She went around exchanging insults with some; others she told, for the first time, that she loved them.

Someone would open the cell door and offer her oranges. Then the door would close again.

When night fell she would sing:

"*Eres alta y delgada* ..." ["You are tall and slim"]

"Sing that again," a voice would ask, from the cell above.

And she would sing it again.

"Thank you," the voice would say.

Every night the voice would ask her to sing that song, and she never saw the face it belonged to.

– 2 –

"It's been several nights now," she tells me, "since I've dreamt about the machine. Since I saw you. You know what? Sometimes I'm afraid to sleep. I know I'm going to dream about that and it scares me. I'm also frightened, still, by footsteps on the stairs. I was awake when they came. I never told you. I heard their steps and I wanted the walls to open up and I thought: I'm going to jump out the window. But I let them take me away.

"'Are you going to talk or not?' they said.

I don't have anything to say.

"'Strip her.'

"They gave me so much electric shock in my mouth my teeth were loosened. And here and here and here. But in the bathtub it's much worse. You know, I could never again swim underwater. I can't stand being without air underwater.

"They pulled off my hood.

"'The boys say you're hot stuff,' the top officer said. 'And I'm going to let them have their fun.'

"A guy came in and got undressed. He flung himself on top of me and started to struggle with me. I looked at what was happening as if I were someone else. I remember that on the radio Palito Ortega was singing. And I told him,

"'You're pathetic. You can't even do it by force.'

"He punched me a few times.

"Another guy came. Big and fat. He took off his plaid shirt and his undershirt.

"'Looks like you're a wild one. With me you're not going to get away with anything.'

"He finished undressing and threw himself over me. He bit my neck and my breasts. I was very far away. I felt cold air escaping from my pores.

"Then the officer in charge came, furious. He kicked me around the floor. He sat on me and buried the butt of his revolver between my legs.

"Later he called me a 'whore' because I didn't cry."

The System

The denunciation of a dictatorship's crimes doesn't end with a list of the tortured, murdered, and disappeared. The machine gives you lessons in egoism and lies. Solidarity is a crime. To save yourself, the machine teaches, you have to be a hypocrite and a louse. The person who kisses you tonight will sell you tomorrow. Every favor breeds an act of revenge. If you say what you think, they smash you, and nobody deserves the risk. Doesn't the unemployed worker secretly wish the factory will fire the other guy in order to take his place? Isn't your neighbor your competition and enemy? Not long ago, in Montevideo, a little boy asked his mother to take him back to the hospital, because he wanted to be unborn.

Without a drop of blood, without even a tear, the daily massacre of the best in every person is carried out. Victory for the machine: people are afraid of talking and looking at one another. May nobody meet anybody else. When someone looks at you and keeps looking, you think, "He's going to screw me." The manager tells the employee, who was once his friend,

"I had to denounce you. They asked for the lists. Some name had to be given. If you can, forgive me."

Out of every thirty Uruguayans, one has the job of watching, hunting down, and punishing others. There is no work outside the garrisons and the police stations, and in any case to keep your job you need a certificate of democratic faith given by the police. Students are required to denounce their fellow students, children are urged to denounce their teachers.

In Argentina, television asks, "Do you know what your child is doing right now?"

Why isn't the murder of souls through poisoning written up on the crime page?

Buenos Aires, January 1976: Introduction to Literatur

I spend the day with Eduardo and my children. I write about sad things. One night I show them to Eduardo. He shoves them aside with a grimace.

"You have no right," he says.

I get angry.

"Why not?"

And Eduardo tells me that on Friday he went to the corner delicatessen near his home to buy ham and salami. The saleswoman is a fat lady who spends her days slicing coldcuts, wrapping packages, adding figures, charging; she minds the shop all alone, and when night comes and she pulls down the metal curtain, she feels pangs in her kidneys and her legs. Eduardo waited his turn, ordered, and paid. Then he noticed that under the cash register drawer was an open book that the saleswoman read out of the corner of her eye as she worked. It was a book I had written.

"I've read it several times," the saleswoman said. "I read it because it does me good. I'm Uruguayan, you know."

And now Eduardo says, "You have no right," as he pushes away the sad, maybe cowardly little things I wrote during those days.

Buenos Aires, January 1976: No One Can Do Anything in the Face of Such Beauty

At the end of the afternoon I sit at a table in the "I Musici" cafe.

Chino Foong, recently arrived from Caracas, shows me some pictures of a mural and paintings he has done which recreate the faces and the themes of da Vinci, Van Gogh, and Matisse. He shows me his latest drawings and silkscreens. He tells me about an exhibition he's planning.

"It's the history of America," says Chino, "seen through the eyes of Botticelli's 'Spring.' "

I look at him.

"Understand? The entire story of the plunderings and the murders through this woman. Because this naked woman is America. Understand?"

And he says,

"When I look at the Mona Lisa, I see her get old. I can turn her into a whore, I can invent another memory for her. But with this woman of Botticelli, just the opposite happens. If I make her older, she doesn't exist.

I isolate the hands, the eyes, a foot, it's no use: there's no way I can hurt her."

I think about the wonder of America in the eyes of the conquerors.

"Charles V was a moment in history and he really couldn't do anything to her," Chino says. "Teddy Roosevelt couldn't do anything. Those here now can't either."

"Everyone pursued her," Chino laughs. "And Columbus, who was the first to enter, died without knowing it."

The Universe as Seen Through a Keyhole

"Every day," Freddy says, "I help prepare the strips of plasticine he uses for writing. He doesn't use paper and pencil. He writes by engraving signs in the plasticine. I can't read what he writes. You can't read what he writes with your eyes. You have to read it with your fingers.

"With him I learned to *feel* a leaf. I didn't know how to. He taught me. 'Close your eyes,' he told me. Patiently he taught me to feel the leaf of a tree with my fingers. It took me a long time to learn because I wasn't used to this. Now I enjoy caressing leaves, letting my fingers slide over the smooth side, feeling the little fuzz on the bottom and the vein-like strands on the inside of the leaf.

"The other day they brought a newborn lion to school. No one could touch it. They just left him alone. And later I asked him,

"'You, who could touch him, can you tell me what the cub was like?'

"'He was warm,' he said, 'and soft.'

"And he asked me,

"'You, who saw him, what was he like?'

"And I told him he was yellow.

"'Yellow? What's yellow like, Freddy?'

"'Like the warmth of the sun,' I told him."

Quito, February 1976: First Night

I switch on the bedlamp for the thousandth time. There is nothing in this hotel which is not an enemy. I toss and turn in the sheets, bury my face in the hot pillow. There is no room in my body for any certainty, no matter how small.

I sleep, somehow, until daybreak.

The telephone's long rings wake me up. I grab the receiver; it falls from my hands. Words come out of it. At last they find my ear.

"Welcome," says the voice. "The city of Quito welcomes you!" I found out just yesterday and said to myself, 'I'm going to call him up to express the satisfaction and the pride that..."

"Sir," I say, or beg, "What time is it, Sir?"

"Seven o'clock exactly," says the voice triumphantly. "In the name of the city of Quito ..."

The receiver dangles over the bedtable.

I try to sleep again. The receiver, swaying on the cord, emits sounds and buzzes. It's no use. I bring my head closer. The words scrape out, slowly.

"I'm sleeping, Sir," I murmur.

"Ah!" exclaims, the voice. "How different the customs of our countries are! But underneath we are united by the same American calling. I will immediately send you a book of mine in which you will note the vibration of ..."

I throw the telephone on the floor, put a pillow and blanket on top of it, and roll over on the bed.

A knock at the door wrenches me out of my second sleep.

I get up, naked, dizzy, and open the door. Vaguely I distinguish something like a bellboy, who places an envelope in my hands and flees.

I slip down against the shut door. My head is splitting. I rub my eyes. The envelope contains several mimeographed copies of a training manual for the Boy Scouts of Ecuador. All of them have a dedication in them to me from the author.

I bury myself in the bathtub. I turn the shower on. I don't know how long I sit there with the rain on my head.

When I'm drying myself I remember to unbury the telephone and put the receiver back on the hook.

Then it rings. I answer. The same voice asks if I have received the package and if I have had a chance to read the book. I tell him I think it is marvelous.

"I'm not going to offend you," I say, "with a purely literary opinion. Works of this kind can be considered neither books nor pamphlets. They are the bricks that are building our Great Fatherland!"

Quito, February 1976: A Talk at the University

Today we have been talking about what they call cultural alienation.

In this country everything revolves around oil now. The banana age has come to an end; it has been promised that in ten years Ecuador will have as much income as Venezuela. This utterly poor country enters the delirium of the millions and gets dizzy. It suffers from vertigo. Before the schools, the hospitals, and the factories arrive, the colored televisions come. Soon there will be electric floor waxers in dirt-floored homes and electric refrigerators in hamlets illuminated by kerosene lanterns. Six thousand liberal arts students and just two students training in petroleum technology; all illusions are allowed in the university, but reality is not possible.

This country is quickly becoming a part of civilization; that is, part of a world in which flavors, colors, smells, as well as words and ideas, are mass produced, and in which the word "Liberty" is the name of a jail, as in Uruguay, and in which an underground torture chamber is called "Dignity Colony," as in Chile. Formulas for sterilizing consciences have more success than birth control programs. Machines for lying, for castrating, for drugging; the media multiply and spread Western, Christian democracy together with violence and ketchup. You don't have to read or write to listen to a transistor radio or to watch television and receive the daily message that teaches you to accept the domination of the strongest and to confuse your personality with an automobile, dignity with a cigarette, and happiness with a hot dog.

We have also talked today about the importation of a false "protest culture" in Latin America. In the developed countries the fetishes and symbols of the youth rebellion of the 1960s in the United States and Europe are being mass produced. Clothes with psychedelic patterns are sold to the cry of "Free Yourself," and big business floods the Third World with music, posters, hairstyles, and apparel that reproduce the aesthetic models of drug hallucinations. Our lands are fertile terrain. To the young people who want to flee from hell, tickets to limbo are offered; the new generations are invited to abandon History, which is painful, and travel instead to Nirvana. Paralytic adventures: reality remains intact, but its appearance is altered. Love without pain and peace without war are offered.

About all of this, and other things, we have talked today.

Esmeraldas, February 1976: Don't You Ever Remember When You Were Born?

– 1 –

They invite me to give a talk on the coast.

I come down from the highlands to the sea. In Esmeraldas they greet me with guitars and firewater. Another world: men with black skin, humid and hot land, women who dance as they walk.

The next night I get lost on the beach. I feel like climbing a high hill and then I begin to follow, through the weeds, a dry riverbed. When I get back it's pitch dark and not a soul is in sight.

I shout out for my friends. Nothing is to be heard but the sound of the sea. I walk along the sand, with no destination or clothes or money. The ferocious mosquitoes are having me for dinner. I'm tired of smacking them with my open hand. I don't have the slightest idea where I am. Every now and then I shout, wait for an answer, go on.

I take off my swimsuit and go into the sea. The water is warm and luminous. When I come out I'm cold. I run and jump in the sand, shadow boxing. The mosquitoes won't leave me in peace. I'm hungry: my stomach growls.

I look for wood to make a fire. I'm busy at this when, from out of the trees, a human being appears. It's a boy who has missed the last bus for Esmeraldas. He looks at me distrustfully. Obliged by the mosquitoes, he draws near the fire. I offer him a cigarette. Later he confesses he's afraid of the wolf dogs and the monkey spiders, of crabs and sharks.

– 2 –

I'm wanting to go to sleep when I hear my friends' voices.

We wake up a Chinese cook in a cabin. We bribe him. He serves us beer and prepares us a giant platter of shrimp in an unforgettable red sauce.

My friends have been hunting for me all afternoon. I then discover that the place where I had gotten lost was known as "Suicide Cliff."

We sleep in some wooden cabins.

– 3 –

When I wake up, the light is about to ignite the blue mountains. I feel the sand slip between my toes. Each grain of sand is alive, each pore of my skin is alive. Good music is born in me.

Quito, February 1976: Introduction to the History of America

There were two neighboring Indian towns. Their livelihood was sheep and what little the land gave them. They cultivated, in terraces, the side of a mountain that drops down to a very beautiful lake near Quito. The two towns had the same name and hated each other.

Between the towns was a church. The priest was dying of starvation. One night he buried a wooden Virgin and sprinkled salt on top. In the morning some sheep dug up the dirt and the Miraculous Virgin appeared.

The Virgin was covered with offerings. From both towns food, clothes, and ornaments were brought. The men of each town prayed for the death of the men of the neighboring town and at night they would stab one another to death. They would say, "It's the will of the Virgin."

Every promise was an act of revenge and thus the two little towns, both called Pucará, exterminated each other. The priest got rich. Everything, the crops and the livestock, ended up at the feet of the Virgin.

Then, for a handful of coins, a multinational hotel chain bought this unpopulated land.

A tourist center is to be built on the lakeside.

Quito, February 1976: Good Will

Margarita, I'm told by Alejandro Adoum, spent some time in Cañar.

In those high plateaus the Indians still wear black because of the crime of Atahualpa. The community shares the little that can be reaped from the arid land.

There are no newspapers; no one knows how to read anyway. There are no radios either; and in any case radios speak the language of the conquerors. How do these little villages learn what is going on in the community? Each village sends two or three actors off on a tour of the region: they act out the news and the problems. In telling what happens to them, they tell what they are:

"They have taken the sun and the moon away from us. They have brought other gods. We don't understand them, but because of them we are killing each other."

Margarita didn't go to Cañar to teach theater, but to learn and help.

The months rolled by. Margarita suffered from the cold and homesickness.

The chief of the community, whose name is Quindi, placed a hand on her shoulder.

"Márgara," he said. "You are very sad. And if you are, it's better you go. We have enough sorrow of our own."

The System

Out of every hundred children born alive in Guatemala or Chile, eight die. Eight also die in the poor outskirts of San Pablo, the richest city in Brazil. Accident or assassination? The criminals have the keys to the jails. This is violence without bullets. No good for murder mysteries. This violence appears frozen into statistics, when it does appear. But the real wars are not always the most spectacular and it's well known that the fire from bullet shots has made more than one person deaf and blind.

Food is more expensive in Chile than in the United States; the minimum wage, ten times lower. A fourth of all Chileans receive no income at all and survive out of sheer stubbornness. The taxi drivers of Santiago no longer buy dollars from tourists. Now they offer girls who will make love in exchange for a meal.

In Uruguay, the consumption of shoes has dropped by 80 percent in the past twenty years. In the last seven years, milk consumption in Montevideo has been halved.

How many prisoners of necessity are there? Is a man condemned to live in pursuit of work and food? How many have their fates written on their faces the day they make their way into the world and cry for the first time? How many are denied sun and salt?

Quito, February 1976: No Rest Until They Fall

This woman has seen her best friend die.

They were occupying a factory in the suburbs of Santiago, Chile, during the days following the coup. They were waiting for weapons, hoping to resist.

They dismembered him under torture, but he didn't say he knew her.

They dragged him over to her. A trail of blood was left in his path. He kept on denying. She heard the officer give the order to shoot him. They threw him against a wall and the policeman stepped back and hesitated. Suddenly he raised his rifle, aimed, and she saw how the head exploded.

Then the policeman screamed, flung down his rifle, and ran out, but he didn't get far. The officer sprayed his waist with bullets and cut him in half.

Quito, February 1976: I Light the Fire and Beckon It

— 1 —

Evening at the home of Ivan Egüez. I start to talk about Roque Dalton.

Roque was a living absurdity who never stopped. Even now, in my memory, he's running. How did death manage to catch him?

They were going to shoot him, but four days before the execution the government fell. Another time they were about to execute him and an earthquake split the prison walls and he escaped. The dictatorships of El Salvador, the little country which was his land and which he carried tattooed all over his body, could never handle him. Death took its revenge on this fellow who had so often mocked it. In the end, it slayed him through treason: it delivered the bullets from the precise place he least expected them. For months no one really knew what had happened. Was it, wasn't it? The teletypes did not vibrate to tell the world about the assassination of this poet who was born in neither Paris nor New York.

He was the most joyful of us all. And the ugliest. There are ugly people who can at least say, "I'm ugly, but symmetrical." Not he. His face was crooked. He defended himself by saying he hadn't been born that way. That's how he'd been left, he said. First a piece of brick hit his nose when he was playing soccer, the result of a doubtful penalty call. Then a rock hit his right eye. Later, a bottle hurled by a suspicious husband. Afterward, the kicks of the Salvadorean military, who didn't understand his passion for Marxism-Leninism. Then, a mysterious beating on a corner of the Mali Strana, in Prague. A band of thugs left him on the ground with a double-fractured jaw and a concussion.

A few years later, during a military maneuver, Roque was running, gun in hand, bayonet fixed, when he fell into a hole. Waiting for him was a huge sow with her newborn piglets. The sow finished off what was left of Roque.

In July 1970 he told me, choking with laughter, the story of the pig, and he showed me an album of comics about the feats of the famous Dalton brothers, movie screen gunslingers, who had been his ancestors.

Roque's poetry was like him: loving, mocking, combative. He had courage to spare, so he didn't need to mention it.

I talk about Roque and I bring him, tonight, to the home of Ivan. None of those gathered here knew him. What does it matter? Ivan has a copy of *Taberna y otros lugares.* I used to have that book as well, back in Montevideo. Leafing through *Taberna* I fail to find a poem I perhaps imagined, but which he could well have written, about the fortune and beauty of being born in America.

Ivan, who knows the Prague tavern "Ufleka," reads a poem aloud. Luis reads a long poem or love story. The book passes from hand to hand. I select some lines that describe how lovely sudden anger can be.

– 2 –

We all meet death in a way that resembles us. Some of us, in silence, walking on tiptoe; others, shrinking away; others, asking forgiveness or permission. There are those who meet it arguing or demanding explanations, and there are those who make their way slugging and cursing. There are those who embrace death. Those who close their eyes; those who cry. I always thought that Roque would meet death roaring with laughter. I wonder if he could have. Wouldn't the sorrow of being murdered by those who had been your comrades have been stronger?

Then the bell rings. It is Humberto Vinueza, coming from Agustín Cueva's house. As soon as Ivan opens the door Humberto says, without receiving any explanation or asking anything, "It was a dissident faction."

"What? How?"

"Those who killed Roque Dalton. Agustín told us. In Mexico the press said ..."

Humberto sits down with us.

We all fall silent, listening to the rain hitting the window.

The Third Bank of the River

Guimarães Rosa had been warned by a gypsy, "You are going to die when you achieve your greatest ambition."

Strange thing: this man of so many gods and demons was the most formal of gentlemen. His greatest ambition was to be made a member of the Brazilian Academy of Letters.

When he was named, he invented excuses to postpone his entrance. For years he invented excuses: health, the weather, a trip …

Until he decided the time had come.

The solemn ceremony was held, and in his speech Guimarães Rosa said, "People do not die. They become enchanted."

Three days later, one Sunday noon, his wife found him dead when she returned home from mass.

I Owe Him a Couple of Stories, Though He Doesn't Know It, and I'm Going to Pay Him

I don't know don Alejo Carpentier.[11] Someday I'll have to go see him. I'll have to tell him.

"Look, don Alejo, I think you probably never heard of Mingo Ferreira. He is a compatriot of mine who draws with grace and drama. He's been with me for years in successive newspaper, magazine, and book adventures. He worked at my side and I knew something about him, though not too much. He's a fellow of few words. What comes out of him are pictures, not words. He's from Tacuarembo, the son of a cobbler; he's always been poor."

And I would tell him,

"In Montevideo he got himself jailed and beaten up several times. One time he was jailed for several months, close to a year, I think, and when he got out he told me that in the place they were locked up they could read aloud. It was a filthy shed. The prisoners were all on top of one another, surrounded by guns, and they couldn't move, not even to urinate. Every day one of the prisoners stood up and read to the others.

"I wanted to tell you, don Alejo, that the prisoners chose to read *El siglo de las luces* [*Explosion in the Cathedral*] and couldn't. The guards allowed the book in, but the prisoners couldn't read it. I mean, they began it several times and had to put it down. You made them feel the rain and smell the violent fragrances of the earth and the night. You brought them the sea and the roar of the waves breaking against the keel of a boat and you showed them the throbbing of the sky at daybreak, and they couldn't keep reading this."

And I would say to him,

"Maybe you remember Milton Roberts. Milton was that big guy with the lovely look in his eyes who interviewed you for *Crisis*. He had gone to Paris, in mid-1975, I think, and I commissioned him to do an interview. Do you remember? Milton had gone to see some French doctors who knew more about his disease. But there was nothing to be done. He returned to Buenos Aires and was soon bedridden. It was a long ordeal. He swelled up. He began to lose his voice. Before the disease entered his throat, Milton spoke to me a few times about the interview. He told me all of it. He remembered everything, word for word. He spoke about you as if you'd been his lifelong friend. He told me your stories about pirates and dictators, one by one, filled with details about the customs and small voices of two or three centuries past. He talked about all of this and his eyes lit up; and it is with this expression that he remains in my memory.

"After he died his compañera, Claudine, went through all his papers looking for the interview notes. She looked and looked, but found nothing. Those papers never turned up."

And tell him,

"I wanted to tell you all these things, compañero Alejo, and give them to you, because they are yours."

Ceremonies of Anguish

– I –

Tough guy, the Old Man. He fends off love. He helped me a lot. I was twenty when I met him. Time passed. I would visit him, bring him what I'd written. He would make faces and give me his implacable opinion; I did what I could to entertain him a bit.

Once, long ago, I dropped by City Hall in search of him. The Old Man had a job there, a bit phantasmagoric: he directed libraries that didn't exist. He worked surrounded by old women functionaries, each uglier than the last, who talked continuously about their money matters and the children. I went over to the counter and waited. The entire harem was present. They sipped maté and ate cookies. At last one of them came over. I asked for him.

"No," said the functionary, taking off her glasses.

She started wiping the glasses with a handkerchief.

"No ..." she said. "He didn't come. He hasn't come in a long time."

"What's the matter?" I asked. "Is he ill?"

She raised her eyebrows in a gesture of compassion. Then she looked at her glasses in the light.

"Poor thing ..." she said. "Poor thing."

And she added,

"You know? He isn't from this world."

– 2 –

I found him sprawled on his bed. He spent long periods like this. On that occasion, in Montevideo, I think he still had the glass by his bed—a complicated mechanism comprised of tubes, coils, and retorts he had brought from Vienna. The apparatus served the purpose of saving the Old Man the effort of pouring his own wine. All he had to do was to move his hand slightly: the glass pressed a valve and was filled up with wine.

During these periods, the Old Man never got out of bed and had nothing to eat. He was organizing himself to die little by little.

"I write in spurts. That urge to write all night, until daybreak, doesn't come anymore."

He drank very ordinary wine, the kind that makes your urine purple, and he gobbled down pills so he could always sleep. But sometimes he was awake and this he called insomnia. By the light of his bed lamp he read murder mysteries that would pile up, mountains of garbage, around his bed. A portrait of Faulkner presided over the head of the bed.

That day, I opened the window and the blinds, without being asked, and the blast of daylight almost killed him. We cursed each other out for a good while. I offered to bring him some bats to complete the atmosphere. I told him jokes and political gossip, which he liked, while he grumbled about the heat or the cold or the light, and I finally got a smile out of him. We discussed, as usual, in the slow and lethargic way he discusses, why I don't think man was and will be worthless and why I don't join him when he invites me along on his journey to the bottom of the pit of hopelessness. I can't fool around with this—if I let myself fall in, I'll stay there. I can't caress death without entering it.

I knew it wasn't a joke. I knew, I know, because I know him and I read him, that the Old Man's bony body is full of demons that harass him and tie him into knots and sink daggers into him and it's to see if he can make them dizzy that he fills his body with wine and smoke, his eyes glued to the moisture stains on the ceiling. To sleep, perhaps to dream, is a ceasefire. The murder mysteries are a cease-fire. Writing, when he manages to, is also a cease-fire, and perhaps the only triumph he is permitted. Then, when he writes, he rises above his filth and ruin and converts them into gold, and he is king.

– 3 –

Sometimes he forgot he was a porcupine. And he said,

"When I was a boy, I was in the Black Pirate band. There was a Sandokan band and there were several others, but I was in the Black Pirates to the end."

"Honorata's sweetheart. I know."

"He was in love with a blond, as far as I know, and it was an impossible love."

"You're wrong. That was the Tiger of Mompracem."

"The Black Pirate, numbskull. The Pirate was crazy about the blond. I should know, I was in the band."

"They're dangerous."

"What?"

"Blonds."

"That blond, Honorata, didn't have anything to do with Sandokan's. You're mixed up. Sandokan operated on Malaysia. The Pirate was from the Caribbean."

"Honorata loved the Black Pirate."

"She loved him all right. But what about the governor of Maracaibo? You think it's just a matter of loving each other? Poor Black Pirate. He had to fall in love with the niece of his mortal enemy."

"In the end, it was death."

"How is he going to die, that bastard?"

"Honorata, I mean. Not the governor. He had lousy health, but he didn't die. Remember? He had gout. He would have evil thoughts, his leg stretched up on a footrest. He didn't die. Honorata did."

"They killed her, you mean."

"Her uncle's soldiers."

"Yes. During the escape."

"Musket shot it was."

"She jumped off the balcony and the Pirate caught her in his arms."

"It entered her chest, here."

"Lower. It went through her scapula."

"Tell me. Have you been in Maracaibo?"

"Yes."

"Tell me about it."

"There are tall buildings, air-conditioned, and a lake full of oil rigs."

"Nitwit. You didn't see anything. Don't you know that in Maracaibo you can't even walk because there are so many ghosts in the streets?"

– 4 –

In mid-1973 they made him a judge in a literary contest and the Old Man crossed the river. One evening he invited me to dinner. He was with a woman. We walked a few blocks, the three of us, in downtown Buenos Aires, in the area the locals call The City. He walked with difficulty, tiring easily. It was hard but he wanted to, and he seemed quite happy, even though he said he didn't recognize the streets and places in that city where he had lived years before.

We went to a place where they served beer, on Lavalle Street. The Old Man ordered a few appetizers and left his utensils crossed over his plate. He was quiet. I ate. She talked.

Suddenly the Old Man asked her,

"Don't you want to go to the ladies room?"

And she said,

"No, no."

I finished my sausage and Russian salad. I called the waiter and ordered a smoked rib of pork with little, round potatoes. Three drafts.

The Old Man persisted.

"But are you sure you don't want to go to the ladies room?"

"Yes, yes," she said. "Don't worry."

A little while later, again.

"Your face is shiny," he told her. "You'd better go to the ladies room to put a little powder on."

She fished out a little mirror from her purse.

"It's not shiny," she said, surprised.

"But I think you really do want to go to the ladies room," the Old Man insisted. "I think you want to go to the ladies room."

Then she reacted.

"If you want to be alone with your friend, tell me, that's all. If I'm a bother, tell me and I'll go."

She was weeping.

"You're not leaving here without eating a dessert. He didn't mean to say that. He wants you to stay."

Unperturbed, the Old Man stared at the gold-colored window curtains.

That was the most difficult dessert of my life. He didn't touch it. She had a little spoonful of ice cream. The fruit salad got stuck in my throat.

Finally she got up. She said good-bye, her voice broken from crying, and she left. The Old Man didn't move a muscle.

He was silent for some time. With a slight nod of his head he accepted coffee.

"You really have to screw yourself," he said at last. "You know why I wanted her to go to the ladies room for a minute? To tell you I feel very happy. To tell you I've never felt better with her than during these days. To tell you I'm a young colt, that ..."

And he shook his head.

"You really have to screw yourself," he said.

The Man Who Knew How to Keep Quiet

Juan Rulfo said what he had to say in a few pages, all bone and meat, with no fat, and then he kept quiet.[12]

In 1974, in Buenos Aires, Rulfo told me he didn't have time to write as he'd like to, due to his workload as a civil servant. In order to have time he needed a leave of absence, and you had to ask doctors for the leave. And you can't, Rulfo explained, go to the doctor and explain, "I feel sad," because doctors don't give leaves for that.

Quito, March 1976: Last Night

The telephone rings. It's time to go. We haven't slept more than a few minutes but feel fresh and wide awake.

We have made love and have eaten and drunk, with the sheet as a tablecloth and our legs as a table, and we have made love again.

She has told me sad things about Chile. It's difficult, she has told me, for companions to be dead after she has seen them so alive. She escaped by the skin of her teeth and now asks herself what she should do with so much freedom and survival.

We arrive at the airport late. The plane has been delayed. We have breakfast three times.

We've known each other a half day.

I walk, without looking back, toward the plane. The runway is surrounded by blue volcanoes. My body's electricity and hunger startle me.

The Universe as Seen Through a Keyhole

When she was small, Mónica didn't want to go out at night, so she wouldn't step on the poor snails. She was also afraid of the trickle of blood dripping down from a truck abandoned on the road and she would lose herself down in the fields, among the weeds.

Mónica fell in love with the baker's son, who was a rascal and hated by all the mothers. She would steal glimpses of him when they were singing the national anthem before entering class. Then the lines would break up and she would crash, poom, right into the bronze bust of Artigas.

Mónica wanted to be a night club dancer as a girl. She wanted to walk around with colored feathers on her bottom and feel like a bird and fly and sin.

Years later, Mónica was one of the few people who went through the trials of horror without drying up or breaking. I liked listening to her. Mónica Lacoste and her companion were my neighbors in Buenos Aires; and their house was always full of Uruguayans.

One midday I went to the market with her. The market, installed in the old railway station, was a festival of aromas and colors and cries: "Give me tomatoes, three, very ripe. Onions, how much will it be? Look, what a lovely lettuce, put it there, and give me a bigger one; oh, garlic and parsley; do you have any peppers? Of course, and what peppers they are; I recommend the green ones; move over, move over, if you don't work you can get out please."

Mónica stuck a couple of radishes in her hair and smiled at everybody. We returned home loaded down with bags and packages.

Pancho, Mónica's son, was behind us, paralyzed by some marvel in the street, like the balustrade of a balcony, a shop window, an iron door, a pigeon eating. He would stand open-mouthed in wonder and we would have to go back to fetch him.

"Let's go Pancho," I said. He asked me to buy him a little toy.

Then he ran ahead to greet the newspaper man, and he offered him a peanut. The newspaper man didn't want it.

"Why don't you want it?" he asked. The newspaper man lowered his head and confessed,

"I'm allergic."

Buenos Aires, March 1976: Shadows and Suns

A man and woman celebrate, in Buenos Aires, thirty years of marriage. They invite other couples from those days, people they haven't seen in ages, and on the yellowed embroidered wedding tablecloth they eat, laugh, toast, drink. They empty quite a few bottles, tell dirty jokes, choke from eating and laughing so much and slapping each other on the back. At some point, past midnight, a silence falls. The silence slips in, settles down, triumphs. Sentences are left hanging in mid-air, laughter is suddenly out of place. No one dares leave. Then, nobody knows how, the game begins. The guests play at who has been dead the longest. They ask each other how many years they have been dead: no, no, they say, not twenty years. You're lowering your age. You've been dead twenty-five years. And so on.

Someone at the magazine told me this story of age and revenge that took place at their home the night before. I had just finished listening to it when the telephone rang. It was a Uruguayan companion I knew slightly. Now and then she would meet me to give me political information or to see what could be done for other exiles without homes or work. But now she wasn't calling about this. This time she called to tell me she was in love. She told me she had at last found what she had been searching for without knowing she had been searching and she needed to tell someone and she was sorry to bother me and that she had discovered she could share her innermost feelings and she wanted to tell me because the news is good, isn't it, and I don't have anyone to tell it to and I thought ...

She told me they had gone to the racetrack together for the first time in their lives and the splendor of the horses and the silk jackets had dazzled them. They had had a little money and had bet with great confidence they would win because it was the first time and they had bet on the nicest horses and the ones with the funniest names. They had lost everything and had walked home absolutely happy with the beauty of the animals and the excitement of the races and because they too were young and beautiful and capable of everything. "Right now," she said, "I'm dying to go out into the street, play the trumpet, hug people, shout that I love him and that it's marvelous to have been born."

This Old Woman Is a Country

– 1 –

The last time Grandmother came to Buenos Aires she came without any teeth, like a newborn baby. Graciela had warned me, by phone, from Montevideo. "She's very worried. She asked me, 'Won't Eduardo find me ugly?'"

Grandmother had become bird-like. The years had been passing and were shrinking her.

We left the port arm in arm.

I suggested we take a taxi.

"No, no," I said. "It isn't because I think you'll get tired. It's because the hotel is very far away, understand?"

But she wanted to walk.

"Look, Grandmother," I said. "It's not worth it here. The scenery is ugly. This is an awful part of Buenos Aires. Afterward, when you're rested, we'll go walk in the parks together."

She stopped, looked me up and down. She insulted me. And she asked, furious,

"Do you think I look at the scenery when I'm with you?"

She hung on to me.

"I feel bigger," she said, "when I'm under your wing."

She asked me, "Do you remember when you carried me in your arms in the sanatorium after the operation?"

She talked about Uruguay, the silence and the fear.

"Everything is so dirty. Everything is so dirty."

She talked about death.

"I'm going to be reincarnated as a thistle. Or as one of your grandchildren or great grandchildren."

"But, Granny," I said. "You're going to live two hundred years. Don't talk to me about death—you have a long time yet."

"Don't be perverse," she said.

She told me she was tired of her body.

"Every now and then I tell my body, 'I can't stand you.' And he answers, 'Neither can I.'"

"Look," she said, stretching the skin on her arm.

She talked about the trip.

"Do you remember when the fever was killing you in Venezuela and I spent the night crying, in Montevideo, without knowing why? These past days I've been telling Emma, 'Eduardo is troubled,' and I came. And now I still think you're troubled."

– 2 –

Grandmother stayed a few days and returned to Montevideo.

After awhile I wrote her a letter. I told her not to take care of herself, not to get bored, not to get tired. I told her I was well aware where the clay I was made of had come from.

And later they told me she had had an accident.

I called her up.

"It was my fault," she told me. "I escaped and went walking to the university, taking the same route I would use to see you. Remember? I know I can't do this sort of thing. Every time I go, I fall. I reached the foot of the steps and said, aloud, 'Aroma del Tiempo,' the name of the perfume you gave me once. And then I fell. They picked me up and brought me here. They thought I had broken a bone. But today, as soon as they left me alone, I got out of bed and escaped. I went out into the street and said, 'I'm very much alive and crazy, like he wants me to be.'"

Buenos Aires, April 1976: The Comrade Walks on Thin Ice

– 1 –

Not long ago he received a phone call from a fellow with an imperious voice. He said he had to see Vicente urgently. At first Vicente did not recognize him. Then he remembered. As a lawyer Vicente had helped him a few years back—some mess with a bounced check. He hadn't charged him anything.

Vicente told him he was going crazy with work and he didn't have a free moment and …

They met in a cafe. The man insisted they drink imported whiskey. Vicente said he didn't want any and at this time of morning …

They drank imported whiskey.

Then Vicente learned that the man was a police officer.

"I'm in the special operations command," the man said, "and I've received an order to kill you."

He told Vicente it would be best if he vanished for a week. The following week he would receive another list, with other names on it. Every week the lists changed.

"I don't guarantee to save your life or anything. I'm just telling you to hide for a week. We have a lot to do. You aren't very important."

Vicente said he thanked him and he didn't know how to ...

"Now we're even," said the man. "I don't owe you anything anymore. You did me a favor two years ago. You're paid. If they give me another order to kill you later and I find you, I'll kill you."

He called the waiter. Without waiting for the change, he arose.

"I'm not going to offer you my hand," he said, "and I don't want to shake yours."

– 2 –

Five years ago, in the Villa Lugano soccer stadium, Vicente Zito Lima made a speech. It was the last day of the political prisoners' hunger strike. Vicente got up on the platform and beyond the crowd he saw Claudia and his daughters playing in the field with the cows and the dogs, and then he forgot the political slogans and started to talk about love and beauty. From below they tugged at his coat, but there was no way to stop him.

– 3 –

Last year we would go to Palermo to play soccer, every Wednesday morning. Behind us, Vicente was lord of the field. Ahead, he attacked everything. I liked to pass him the corners so he could shoot them in with his head. "Good, Eduardo," he would always yell, even when I, clumsy from birth, would mess up the easy goals.

Sometimes we would leave the dressing room together. He told me about his grandfather, the cobbler, anarchist, good with knives and cards, who at the age of seventy ran after girls in the streets.

– 4 –

We don't play soccer anymore.

The team broke up.

Together with Fico and me, Vicente runs the magazine. Now and then we go out for a pizza, because it helps to not think that every night may be the last. Vicente knows the best pizza restaurants in every neighborhood in Buenos Aires.

"In that one, sit near the oven in the back, not the one in front, and ask for a half dough pizzeta, well cooked on the bottom, with Roquefort, tomatoes, and onions. Tell me what you think later."

The knowledge comes from his student days, when he made the rounds of pizzerias in Buenos Aires selling rotten mozzarella that a friend made. The good restaurants are those that didn't buy his cheese.

The other evening we went out for pizza together. Vicente was sad. Buried somewhere in that morning's papers was the news of the death of a militant Vicente had defended. The body had been found in a swamp, together with that of his small son. His name was Sebastián. His wife, Diana, had been murdered four months earlier.

"You know what the happiest day of my life was?" Vicente said. "The day I managed to arrange for them to be together in a court in Buenos Aires. They had been in prison two years without seeing one another. When he was sent to the north, she went south. When she was sent to the provinces, he would be put in Devoto [a prison in Buenos Aires]. At last I managed to get them together, under a legal pretext. I never saw anyone kiss like they did."

The System

The machine persecutes the young: it locks them up, tortures them, kills them. They are the living proof of its impotence. It expels them: it sells them, human flesh, cheap labor, abroad.

The sterile machine hates everything that grows and moves. It is only able to multiply the jails and the cemeteries. It can produce nothing but prisoners and cadavers, spies and police, beggars and exiles.

To be young is a crime. Reality commits it each day, at dawn; and so does history, which is each morning born anew.

And so reality and history are banned.

Chronicle of a Flight over the Purple Land

– I –

The clouds formed a prehistoric turtle.

The waitress brought us coffee. A little light went on and we heard a bell; a voice ordered us to adjust our seatbelts. We'd entered an air pocket. The coffee jostled on the trays. We didn't bother with the belts. As usual, we drank the coffee black; it wasn't bad. Eric sat by the window, looking out.

On the Buenos Aires-bound plane rode a batallion of tourists. They were armed with cameras and flash equipment and home movie cameras. The cargo section was stuffed with empty suitcases which would return to Rio or São Paulo bulging with leather jackets and other trophies from the hunt. I knew the scene well. Tourists.

"Now I understand," I said, "why airplanes carry puke bags."

Eric looked out the window of the Boeing. He glanced at his watch and said,

"This is your land."

We were breaking through a cloud bank. The plane would not stop in Montevideo; it was flying straight on to Buenos Aires.

Below us spread the deserted fields; devastated land, violated land, land unloved by its owners. There below the shepherds on horseback had risen in rebellion. There a *caudillo* in a frayed poncho had decreed the first agrarian reform in Latin America more than a century and a half ago.[13] Reference to this is forbidden in the schools today.

"We're flying over your country," Eric said.

I said,

"Yes."

Eric fell silent.

And I thought: Will this land of mine remember me?

– 2 –

I had returned, by night, frequently. After calling on sleep for a long time in my home in Buenos Aires my eyes would close and the lights of Montevideo would light up: I was walking along the *rambla* by the sea, or along the streets in the center of town, half hidden, half hunted down, looking for my people. Then I would wake up bathed in sweat and choked by the anguish of returning and not being recognized. Then I would get up and go to the bathroom. I would wet my head and drink water from the tap. Then I would go back and stay on the bed, sitting, my chin on my knees. I smoked and thought. Why didn't I return this very day to the place I belonged? My country was broken, and I, prohibited. I knew that I had had more luck than my friends who had been caged or murdered or smashed under torture, and that the prohibition was, in a way, an honor: the proof that writing hadn't been a useless passion. But I would think, "Do I deserve to be here? Am I worth something to someone? Is there an echo or a trace of us in the empty streets of my city? What can I do there, except keep quiet or rot in jail for no reason or just in case?"

The sun would slip into my room in Buenos Aires and I would get up, still sleepy, aching all over, before the alarm rang. I would shower and dress and close the door of the elevator and continue thinking: And if we were a broken rock? A rock that broke, pieces of one sole rock rolling around? Wanderers condemned to be forever just passing through. (A glass of cane brandy on the sideboard. Who is the glass waiting for, whose mouth? An old woman fills it up again each time it evaporates.)

Would I be able, sometime, to purge myself of the doubts that were poisoning my blood? I wanted to exchange all my nights of insomnia and grogginess for the melody the prisoner searches for alone in his cell or the little whiff of happiness awaited by a woman, her head buried in her hands, in a filthy kitchen. I wanted to cross the river and the customs offices and arrive in time. (A boy, dragged by the police, rolls down the stairs. A crowd of old people look on, motionless. The child raises his mud-splattered face. Hate burns in his eyes.)

One of those mornings, as I was walking to the magazine, I remembered a Polish film I had seen years ago. The film described the escape of a group of men through the Warsaw sewer system during the war. They all went underground together. Just one managed to survive. Some got lost in the filthy labyrinths; others fell victims to hunger or were suffocated by the gases. I remembered the face of the survivor, when he finally opened the hatch and emerged from the shadows and the shit: he blinked, wounded by the daylight and stunned by the world. Then he closed the hatch over his head and sank back into the sewer where his dead companions lay. This immolation had had a great impact on me, and I had been indignant at the reaction of the public, which had not understood the great gesture and had yelled at the screen, "Jerk, sucker, what are you doing, you must be an imbecile, you fucking idiot!"

A long time had passed since the night I had seen this film in a neighborhood theater in Montevideo. That morning, walking along the streets of Buenos Aires, I discovered that the public had been right. Those people in the movie house had known more than I, even though they had no idea who Andrej Wajda was and couldn't care less.

— 3 —

Eric dozed beside me on the airplane and my head was buzzing.

When I return, I thought, I'm going to go back to the places where I made myself or was made; and I'm going to repeat, alone, everything that the first time around, once, I experienced in the company of those who are no longer here.

A voice inside me sang the Milton Nascimento song,

"*Descobri que minha arma e*
o que a memoria guarda ..."
["I discover that my strength
is what my memory holds ..."]

Taste of the first milk from the mother's breast. What delicacies could be compared to those chocolates Grandmother bought me in the bakery next door? And the lentils she made every Thursday until I left Montevideo? I'm still pursuing their taste on tables all around the world.

"*Descobri que todo muda e*
que tudo é pequeño ..."
"I discover that everything
changes, that everything is small ..."]

I am going to go to the patio of the house where I learned to walk by holding onto our dog Lily's tail. She was a mongrel, a street dog, which is why no one had bothered to dock her. She had a long tail, a sweet, bleary-eyed expression, and a belly always full of puppies. She slept under my crib and showed her fangs to anyone who wanted to come near. At night the neighborhood dogs howled outside the house gates and bit each other to death over her. Lily taught me to walk, with patience and much rumbling.

I will return to the streets leading down to the sea, which were once open space, the battlegrounds and soccer fields of my first years. That's where we waged war with sticks and stones. We painted horrific eyes and gullets on palm tree trunk bark, which we used as shields. Going out to buy ravioli was an adventure. You had to cross enemy territory. In those empty fields by the coast my teeth got crooked and my brother just missed losing one eye. Mother, who didn't have time for complaints, would cure our wounds; she taught us to bite hard and stand up for ourselves. My brother Guillermo, who never talked much, fought in defense of the rights of birds and dogs.

He never got on in the city. I never saw him happy there. Cities made him sad, swallowed him up; only in the Paysandú fields was he himself.

"*A maior das maravilhas foi ...*"

["The most marvelous thing was ..."]

I'll go horseback riding through the Arroyo Negro grassland, where I learned to gallop. From the time we were quite small my brother and I would race. On Sunday afternoons we would escape from our nap, practically naked, and with one jump we would be clinging to the manes of the barebacked, bitless horses: I flew, and inside me beat the animals' veins, thunder of hoofs, wet hide smell, seething sweat, communion with that force that entered the wind: when I got down, my knees were trembling. My child's wonder would last until night.

Many years later I can recognize this violent happiness, as one recalls one's own birth or the first light. It happens sometimes in the sea, when I go in naked and feel I belong to it. And it happens when I touch a woman and I give birth to her and she brushes against me and creates me, and I enter her and the two of us are immortal for a little while, the two of us are many, in the soaring flight.

– 4 –

I am going to go back to Pepe Barrientos' ranch, in the Buceo.

When the going got tough, Pepe managed to find me a corner in that house. He opened his door and sat me at his table, beside his family.

One morning, Jorge Irisity, who worked with us in the unions, came by. He stopped his car in front of the door and honked the horn for me. From the other side of the wire fence he yelled that Cuba had been invaded. Pepe turned the radio on immediately. The news bulletin announced the victory of the Playa Girón [Bay of Pigs] invasion. My tongue dried up. I drank water all afternoon and there was no way to prevent that burning. At work that afternoon a piece of skin fell off my tongue. Pepe wanted to take me to the doctor. The tongue cured itself.

The years passed. Pepe and I shared some adventures. One summer night we were sitting on the dock in the little port at Buceo, and he asked me what I was up to. He told me there wasn't enough bread in the whole world to appease my hunger.

– 5 –

The voice announced that we would be landing in Ezeiza.

Eric shook me. He thought I was sleeping.

The sun was setting on the river. There was an innocent light, the kind that only appears when days are born or end.

We walked toward a taxi, our suitcases in our hands. For an instant I felt happy and had the urge to jump.

The car slipped down the river drive and then sank into the city.

The Children

By the shore, where the coast opens up and the river becomes ocean, my children were made. Verónica, in the old Buceo inlet, sheltered by some fallen tree trunks. Claudio, on the south side of town. Florencia, on the Atlántida beach.

Graciela and I had taken the bus to the Atlántida casino. Our money wouldn't get us to the end of the month, as usual, and that time, fed up with poverty, we decided to gamble the rest.

We bought a return ticket, just in case. If we won, we would spend the weekend in a good hotel and then we could get to the end of the month without selling our reserves of art books and used bottles. If we lost, we'd sleep on the beach.

We bet on several numbers: 17, 24, 32.... We tried with zero. Chances. Colors, streets, pictures. We didn't understand half of what was going on.

In thirty minutes our pockets were empty.

Then we took a dip in the sea and slept in each other's arms on the sands of Atlántida.

The Children

Verónica and I write each other violent letters.

Sometimes there were long silences. Each of us waited for the other to get down off his high horse—and deep down we each knew the other wouldn't get down. A matter of style.

Verónica lights her cigarette like Humphrey Bogart. She holds the match while she talks about anything, absent-mindedly, looking the other way, and when the flame is already burning her fingernails she slowly draws it up to the cigarette. She lifts an eyebrow, strokes her chin, and extinguishes the match with a puff of smoke blown from the side of her mouth.

When she was visiting me in Buenos Aires she said,

"If you and I weren't father and daughter, we would have separated a long time ago."

One night she went out on the town with Marta and Eric.

Verónica took her rag doll, which she calls Anonymous.

When she woke up, after 12 noon, she told me, "We were hanging out. We went to the 'Bárbaro' and drank beer and ate peanuts. The night was lovely. Luckily we got the table by the window. There was good music."

"And Anonymous?"

"We hung her up on a hook, on the wall, and we ordered beer for her too. The beer made her sleepy."

"Did you stay late?"

"We were loving each other," she said, "until three in the morning."

The Children

Eleven years ago, in Montevideo, I was waiting for Florencia at the door of our building. She was quite small, and walked like a little bear. I didn't see much of her. Until late at night I stayed at the newspaper, and in the mornings I worked at the university. I didn't know much about her. I kissed her when she was asleep; sometimes I brought her chocolates or toys.

Her mother wasn't home that afternoon and I waited at the door for the bus that would bring Florencia home from the nursery.

She arrived in a very bad mood. She didn't speak. In the elevator her face puckered up. Then she let her milk get cold in the cup. She looked at the floor.

I sat her on my knees and asked her to tell me about it. She shook her head. I caressed her, kissed her on the brow. A tear escaped. I dried her face with my handkerchief and she blew her nose. Then I asked her again.

"Come on, tell me."

She told me her best friend had told her she didn't like her.

We cried together, I don't know for how long, there in the chair.

I felt the hurt that Florencia was going to suffer through the years and I would have liked God to exist and not be deaf so I could beg him to give me all the pain he had reserved for her.

The Children

– 1 –

Álvaro, Claudio's best friend, invites him to his beetle circus shows. Claudio told me what the circus was like. There is a grass ring surrounded by a clothespin fence. With wires, little pieces of wood, and string, Álvaro invented a number of games that beetles like. The poor bugs are awkward, in their warriors' armor, but Claudio has seen them, in Álvaro's circus, pirouetting in grand style: they balance on trapezes, jump the fatal jump, go around in a little carriage, and greet the public.

– 2 –

One night Álvaro stayed overnight with Claudio. The next morning their beds were still made and they were exhausted and were dressed.

Claudio explained:

"We opened the window. There was a full moon. We spent the whole night singing and telling stories and talking about girlfriends and things."

– 3 –

Claudio will drink his soup, but with his fork.

He likes to decipher enigmas and to get lost.

"Lovely park to get lost in," he remarks.

And he asks,

"What time is it, Papa? Are the Three Marys in the sky? And the Southern Cross? Isn't it true that everything we invent has already been invented by he who invented us?"

– 4 –

When he was three years old Claudio was weak. Then he entered death and emerged from it.

He panted, his head was afire, and he would make his way as best he could between suffocation and fever and he would smile with clenched teeth.

"I'm all right, Mama," he would stammer. "Don't you see I'm all right?"

He had almost stopped breathing when he got to the hospital, but he revived in the oxygen tent. He traveled to the moon in the oxygen tent, through the fresh, blue universe.

"We astronauts don't use pacifiers," he said when offered one.

"Horses gallop in the sky," he murmured.

Later they put him on the cot to wheel him to the operating room. On the long cot he seemed smaller still. He said good-bye and thank you very much to everyone, one by one, and the elevator door closed.

When the anesthesia wore off he was ravenous.

"I want to eat teeth," he said, half-dazed. He wanted to sit up and couldn't. When he could, he drew a chicken on the sheet.

It took awhile for his lungs to recover fully. He would stick a pencil in his mouth and explain,

"I'm a little man. I smoke and cough. This is why I have such a cough and I cough."

They let him out. He was no longer afraid. He slept without his pacifier and never wet his sheets again.

Buenos Aires, May 1976: Is He Dead? Who Knows?

– I –

We heard the sound of the motor growing louder from afar. We were standing on the pier, waiting. Haroldo balanced the lantern on one arm; the other was wrapped around Marta, who was shivering from the cold.

The searchlight penetrated the fog and found us.

We jumped onto the launch.

For an instant I was able to see the ramshackle boat, pulling the line taut; then the fog swallowed it. In this boat I had rowed, until nightfall, to the island where the store was.

The vaporous fog rose up from the dark river.

It was very cold on the launch. The passengers' teeth chattered. The cold was especially piercing because the night was almost over. We went up a narrow stream, then another, wider one, and we came out into the river. The first rays of light were breaking through the silhouettes of the poplars. The faint light was denuding the little wooden houses half eaten away by the high tides, a white church, the rows of trees. Bit by bit the crests of the cassowaries were illuminated.

I got up on the bow. There was a clean smell. The fresh breeze hit my face. I amused myself looking at the slice of foam following the launch and the growing shine of the river waves.

Haroldo had come over to stand at my side. He made me come back and I saw it: an enormous copper sun was invading the mouth of the river.

We had been spending a few days on the delta, far up, and we were returning to Buenos Aires.

– 2 –

Few people knew this world of the Paraná like Haroldo Conti.[14] He knows the good fishing spots and the shortcuts and the forgotten corners of the islands; he knows the pulse of the tides and the lives of each fisherman and each boat, the secrets of the region and the people. He knows how to get around in the delta the way he knows how to travel, when he writes, through the tunnels of time. He wanders around the streams or sails for days and nights on the open river, searching for that ghost ship he sailed on once in his childhood or in his dreams. While he pursues what he lost, he listens to voices and tells stories to people like him.

– 3 –

A week ago today they dragged him out of his house. They put a blindfold over his eyes and beat him and took him away. Their guns had silencers. The house was stripped bare. They stole everything, even the blankets. The newspapers didn't print a word about the kidnapping of one of the best Argentine novelists. The radios said nothing. Today's paper publishes the complete list of earthquake victims in Udine, Italy.

Marta was at home when it happened. They blindfolded her as well. She had been allowed to say good-bye and had been left with the taste of blood on her lips.

It's been a week since they took him and I no longer have a way to tell him I love him and that I never told him this out of shame or laziness.

Buenos Aires, May 1976: That Voice that Can Withstand Tight-Reined Emotion

Alfredo Zitarrosa sings without quavers or embellishment, macho voice born to name love, which is always dangerous, and to honor men. Tonight I went to his house. There were people there I didn't know.

Alfredo had had a headache for years. No doctor has been able to do anything about it. That ache of the country:

"I'm drunk," he told me.

He talked about other things and interrupted himself to explain to me,

"I'm drunk. This has happened to me a lot."

He asked about Haroldo three times.

"I found out the other day," he told me. "Isn't there anything that can be done for him?"

He served me wine. He sang without really wanting to. In a corner, someone told jokes and laughed by himself.

"I hadn't read anything by Haroldo," Alfredo said. "I bought a book the other day. I like this fellow. Isn't there anything I can do for him?"

He sat for a while, strumming the guitar, his eyes fixed on the floor, and then persisted,

"I thought that novel, *Sudeste*, was very good. I hadn't heard about it because I've read very little, really, and I never knew him either. I knew he was your friend, but I never met him. And now … Can't anything be done?"

He drank the last drop from his glass and then said,

"So nothing can be done for him."

He shook his head. The others started singing a *milonga*. They got halfway through it.

Alfredo looked at me accusingly.

"I don't have your address," he said.

"I'm never at home," I explained.

"You haven't given me your address," he said. "I have the magazine telephone number, but I don't have your address. You didn't give it to me."

"I'll write it down for you."

He passed me a little black book.

I flipped over the pages looking for the index and without wanting to found the agenda page corresponding to the day before.

The others talked quietly.

I read in the agenda:

"Rehearsal.

Record at ION.

Call Eduardo.

Decide to leave."

Do Cities Exist? Or Are They Vapors that Come Out of People's Mouths?

– I –

Under which streets would I like to lie when I'm sent to die? Underneath whose treading? Whose footsteps would I like to hear forever?

What is Montevideo but the sum of people I loved and hated in her and of so much given and received? My furies and sorrows come from these men and these women. They are my national history.

When Emilio offered me a mural for my room in Buenos Aires I asked him to paint me a port in vivid colors. A Montevideo port to arrive at, not depart from: to say hello, not good-bye.

He painted it for me and there it remains.

– 2 –

At siesta time, prisoners in our room, my brother and I had our ears cocked to the voices of the street, which beckoned us. In those days the city had another music: we heard the hoofs of the horses that pulled the ice-cart and the knife sharpener's whistle, and the triangle of the pastry-stick vendor, the ice cream man's cry and the barrel-organ of the little green parrot that told fortunes with its beak.

At our mother's slightest carelessness, we would escape. We would go through the streets throwing pebbles at our friends' windows. When the gang was gathered, we went off to smoke cornsilk cigars in deserted fields. The filthy fish of the ravines were more delicious than family lunches and better than movies were fires built in the shelter of the coastal woods, where we grilled and ate a stolen sausage. Everyone had the right to one bite. Our day's booty oozed droplets of boiling grease and flooded our mouths.

– 3 –

We waited for the summer, and in the summer, party time, carnival.

The eucalyptuses blossomed, Mars shone red in the sky, and the hot earth was warm with little toads.

We roamed the quarries in search of good clay for mask making. We would knead the molds—pointed noises, bulging eyes—and dip them in plaster. We would shape the masks with wet newspaper and then Aunt Emma would help us paint them. We would hang an old pot around our necks and the masked orchestra would set out to wander around the carnival parade.

Every neighborhood had a stage, sometimes two. Among the gigantic colored dolls the carnival groups sang at night.

In the shadows under the stage, with the commotion above, the first little kisses happened.

– 4 –

What happened to the city where the poet Parilla and the painter Cabrerita shared a single suit and took turns using it?

What has replaced "La Telita"? Lito, so fat he slept sitting down, kept guard at the door, a *Toscano* [small cigar] in his mouth. I was fourteen when I went for the first time. I was lucky. I must have looked inoffensive, because the fat guard let me in.

"You, kid, go on in."

Lito's brother, Rafa, kept the clients' accounts on the wall. When the wall was whitewashed the debtors were forgiven, which must have been why they never painted it.

Every night there was wine and guitars, sausages and cheese.

We would sit down to drink and chat on top of the boxes that the next day were filled with tomatoes, lettuce, onions, and oranges. "La Telita," in the heart of Ciudad Vieja, was a wine bar by night and a fruit and vegetable store by day.

It was there I learned the songs of the Spanish Civil War and some Uruguayan tunes I still remember. And I also learned other things, from the mouths of the poets and the sailors.

– 5 –

All the drunks were ardent supporters of freedom of expression. "Me, keep quiet?" they would say. "Me, keep quiet? Do you know who you are addressing at this precise moment of present existence?"

They would argue in loud voices; you could go about the streets without identification papers on you; nobody was afraid.

The Spanish Republicans would meet in the "Sorocabana" at Plaza Libertad. They would quarrel with one another just like in the war, but later they would depart arm in arm. The politicians and theater folk preferred the "Tupí Nambá." We reporters would occupy the "Palace" when the pensioners went off to bed. I was the owner of a table by the window.

The midday gin fizz was consumed at the "Jauja" and the *uvita* [Uruguayan brandy] at the "Fun Fun" in the old market. The "Boston" belonged to the musicians and dancers. In the "Británico," chess and dominoes were played. The Catalonians, the Socialists, and the deaf each had their own cheering sections. When someone had been a customer for thirty years, the "Británico" retired him. From that day on he could get his drinks free.

I had kept these places intact in my memory, complete with their small wooden or marble tables, their buzz of conversation, golden shadows, smoke-blue air, aromas of tobacco and freshly made coffee: they heroically resisted the invasion of acrylic and formica and then at last they were vanquished.

The "Monterrey," which was also off Plaza Independencia, never closed. You ate their flans with soup spoons and you could order dinner at breakfast time, after a night of wine and singing, before going off to work.

Sitting up by the window at the "Monterrey," Gloria whispers tangos, in the early hours, with her hoarse little voice. You could hear a fly. (Gloria loved a man called Maia, who worked on the local ships. One night the love ended and she killed him and herself. They had a wake for her on a table. One thick candle burned at each end.)

Dreams

I would tell you stories about when I was small and you would see them happen in the window. You saw me as a child wandering about the fields and you saw the horses and the light and everything moved softly.

Then you would pick up a shiny green pebble from the window and squeeze it in your fist. From that moment on it was you who were playing and running in the window of my memory, and you would gallop across the fields of my childhood and of your dream, with my wind in your face.

The Universe As Seen Through a Keyhole

I remember the day the violence began.

My brother Guillermo was playing with Gallego Paz on the sidewalk outside our house on Osorio Street.

It was a summer noon.

Seated on the railing, I watched them kick the cloth ball.

Gallego, who was older than we, had a reputation as a fighter and was a gang leader. The other boys made way for him when he showed up in nearby neighborhoods.

There was a questionable goal or something, and fists began to fly. My brother was on the ground and Gallego, who had him pinned down with his knees, was hitting him from above.

I watched him hit without moving or saying anything.

Then suddenly something like a trigger clicked inside me and clouded my vision and I lunged and fell upon him.

I wasn't sure what happened next. They told me that there was a shower of punches and kicks and butts and that I clung to Gallego's neck like a mad dog and there was no way to pull me off.

I remember that I was quite surprised listening to all of this afterward, as if hearing about someone else, while I trembled and licked the blood off my knuckles.

The Universe As Seen Through a Keyhole

One rainy morning in the home of my friend Jorge, we were playing "Ludo"—a dice game—or checkers and then, I don't know how, I was in his older sister's bedroom and lifted up a fistful of her clothes that I had discovered on the bed among the sheets she had mussed and were still warm from her sleep. I felt the startled gaze of God upon me.

Buenos Aires, May 1976: Introduction to Political Economy

Do the economic minister's decrees refer to currency rates, the tax structure, price policies? Why don't they ever mention things like life, death, or destiny? Who is wiser, the person who can read palms or the person who can understand what these decrees are saying without saying it?

One fine day Carlitos Domínguez' father decided to play his last card. His children were grown and didn't need him much. He sold his house—a large one—in order to buy an apartment and a car.

"I'll get the old lady out of the kitchen," he said, "and we'll enjoy life."

They had never traveled. They were going to cross the Andes. What would this be like? How would it feel to be so high up?

Carlitos' father signed the papers selling his house and that same day the minister of economy passed a decree. The papers published it the next day. With the money from the sale of his house, Carlitos' father was able to buy a tiny apartment and nothing else. The little bit of money left over just covered his funeral costs.

When he was in the hospital, Carlitos would visit him and he would beg his son to pull out his I.V.

"I know how you feel," Carlitos would say, "but I don't know how it is done."

His mother never got to know her new neighborhood. She walked into the apartment, tripped, and had a bad fall. She never wanted to get up again.

"I see big black starfish," she said. "They have enormous eyes." Later a gust of wind collapsed the patio roof and nobody ever put it up again. The pictures began falling off the walls. The refrigerator stopped working. The washing machine broke. The telephone went dead.

Carlitos walked into that dark trap of a house and read the letters they wrote to one another before he was born.

The System

There is only one thing which is free: prices. In our countries Adam Smith needs Mussolini. Freedom of investment, freedom of prices, free exchange rates: the freer the businesses, the more imprisoned are the people. The prosperity of a few is everyone else's curse. Who knows of wealth that is innocent? In times of crisis, don't the liberals become conservative, the conservatives fascist? In whose interests do the assassins of people and countries carry out their tasks?

Orlando Letelier wrote in *The Nation* that the economy is not neutral, nor are the technicians. Two weeks later, Letelier was blown to bits on a Washington street. The theories of Milton Friedman gave him the Nobel Prize; they gave Chile General Pinochet.

A Uruguayan economics minister declared, "Inequality in the distribution of income generates savings." At the same time he confessed he was horrified by torture. How can this inequality be maintained if not through jolts of electric shock? The Right loves abstract ideas. By generalizing, it absolves.

Buenos Aires, May 1976: A Bomb on the Desk

— 1 —

Someone is announced.

"Sr. Castro," I'm told.

I step outside my office. In the waiting room is a young man with a package on his knees. He jumps up and embraces me without letting go of the package. I don't recognize him. He says we have to talk—alone.

We go inside my office and I shut the door. He sits in front of me and looks at me.

"I'm listening," I say.

"I'm Uruguayan," he tells me. "Like you."

"That's good," I say.

"Do you know what I have here?" he says, pointing to the package.

"I haven't the slightest idea."

He rests the package carefully on the table and leans so close his face brushes mine.

"It's a bomb."

I jerk back. Castro sits down again. He smiles.

"A bomb," he repeats.

I look out of the comer of my eye at the door. I confirm it is useless to have a pistol tucked away in a drawer.

"I'm with the poor. I'm on the side of the people, I am," Castro tells me. "And you?"

"Absolutely," I assure him.

He places his hand on the package and offers, "Do you want me to open it?"

Out of the package pops a mountain of typewritten pages.

"A bomb," Castro proclaims, euphorically. "This novel will topple the government!"

– 2 –

I console myself by recalling that it is not my first madman.

When we were publishing *Época* in Montevideo, a giant made the rounds of the newspaper offices. He escaped from the asylum each week and walked into the newsrooms, an overpowering presence in his gray-striped overalls and his shaved head, and he would sit on any desk he pleased, threatening, "I'm going to break everything." We knew what to do: he would lie face down on a table and we would scratch his back. Then he would smile, beatific, and leave.

Another madman would come to denounce the sabotage of imperialism: every time he turned on the tap in his bathroom ants would come out. Another, who was a sculptor, had the habit of breaking little angels to bits in the city plazas. He would arrive at any time of night with the wings or the little bronze or marble hands under his jacket, to ask for refuge at the organ of popular causes. And the inventors? There was a short Italian who walked around with a huge roll of paper under his arm. It was the blueprint of a cannon that put out fires where no water was available, by shooting dirt and sand over the flames.

- 3 -

When Achával was literary director of EUDEBA, the university publishing house of Buenos Aires, he received a visiting card from a gentleman who was gray at the temples and wearing a custom-made suit.

The gentleman had brought the manuscript of an unpublished novel.

"I'm the author of this book," said the gentleman, "and I brought it because it is going to be published here."

"Well ..." Ácha hesitated. "We thank you very much for having bothered. Our advisors will see if ..."

"There's nothing to see," the gentleman smiled. "If I tell you that you are going to publish it, it's because you are going to publish it."

Acha nodded his head understandingly. He said that he also hoped it could be published and he would take great pleasure in considering it ...

"Perhaps I haven't made myself clear," the gentleman said.

"Yes, yes," Acha replied. He explained that each series had its own director and advisors and no decision could be taken without ...

"I've already told you that I've brought my novel because it is going to be published here," the gentleman repeated, calmly, and Achával calmly told him that EUDEBA published university texts, that the publishing house had been created for this purpose, and that works of fiction were part of collections for students or of series aimed at the popular dissemination of classical, national, and universal literature, but that at any rate he would do all he could to ...

"Mr. Achával," said the gentleman, "I thank you for your explanation. As I said before, I have brought my novel to this publishing house because I know it will be published here."

Acha looked at him. He swallowed. He lit a cigarette. Then he asked softly,

"And could you tell me who told you it is going to be published here?"

"God told me," the gentleman answered.

"Who?"

"God. He appeared three days ago and said, 'Just take it, it will be published.'"

Claromeco, May 1976: Homage to a Man I Didn't Know

– I –

The snail gatherer can be seen from here. How long have I let my legs carry me onward? What little remains of the sun is fading.

Gulls screech in the sky. Their shadows move in front of me.

I reach Cristián's monolith and read the inscription, which I know by heart. I stand before the stone. Every time I come here I take this long walk in spite of myself.

These footprints of mine were first left by him and were erased, years ago, by this wind and this sea. On other afternoons I felt that he was, as I feel that I am, this bird flying above my head and gliding above the dunes and letting itself drop, head first, into the sea.

No one knows how old Cristián reached these beaches, but stories are told. They say he escaped, swimming, from a Danish ship that was sailing along the coast. He was a great swimmer, they say. He lived off what he fished and the nutrias he caught in the stream. He never let the sea swallow a line: he swam out to wherever it was necessary and untangled the line with his hands or his teeth. It was also claimed that no policeman could ever lay a hand on him.

He was always ready to do a favor, without accepting anything in return, and he had saved some men from death. He gave everything away and never had anything. He had invented a thirty-peso prize for the best student in the region.

Lola the mare helped him throw out the line. By night, old Cristián would do the rounds of the town cafes. The six greyhounds and Lola the mare would wait for him at the door of the cafes. When he was thoroughly drunk, someone would hoist him up on the mare's back so she could take him, along this coast, to the tin shack he had made for himself here on the dunes. The mare would jostle him along on her haunches, swaying with the lurching of his body. Sometimes the old man would slip off and sprawl on the sand. Then the greyhounds would lie down on top of him and sleep on his body, so the frost wouldn't kill him.

I know no more about him than what is told and what a photograph of his bony face and sweet gaze once told me, and what I learn by following his path. I know he never knew a woman, but perhaps, when he drank until he collapsed, he greeted or cursed from afar the girl to whom he had given so much he had been drained dry.

– 2 –

Huge snails and things washed up by the sea appear on these sand banks after storms. The weather has been calm these past days. I don't find anything on the sand or rocks. I pick up, over there, the remains of black glass. It comes from a bottle that the tide smashed against the rocks.

Yala, May 1976: Street War, Soul War

– 1 –

Héctor Tizón was in Europe.[15] He wasn't happy there. He has returned to Yala. These are hard times, but he is sure he is like the land he walks upon.

It's been over a year since we've seen one another. I arrive at Yala with a headache. My neck has been burning for a fortnight.

We walk down the path that leads to the river.

The river bears the name of the town. It is noisy and runs over colored stones. In the spring it drains the ice from the mountains. By night guitars sleep on the banks of the Yala. Their owners leave them there so the little mermaids will tune them.

"We've all been given conditional freedom," Héctor says.

"I'm getting to be the only one around," he says.

The fear is the worst news. "At the funeral of Alberto Burnichón, in Córdoba," Héctor tells me, "there were no more than twelve people."

I had also known this innocent tradesman in unsellable works of art, who roamed the prairies and mountains with armloads of drawings and poetry. Burnichón knew the country rock by rock, person by person, the taste of the wines, the memory of people. They smashed his skull and chest with Itaka shots and they threw him down a well. Not even the ashes were left of his dynamited house. The plates and the books he had published by himself, works of young people from the provinces which he thought showed talent or were gripping, ended up overnight in the basements of bookstores or bonfires. Twenty-five years of work wiped out in one stroke. The murderers have been successful.

"At the funeral there was just one man," says Héctor. "Eleven women and one man."

The worst news is the fear. A couple who are his friends, he tells me, threw their books into their wood stove. One by one, all of their books: a ritual of the times. They began with Lenin and finished off with *Alice in*

Wonderland. When there was nothing left to throw into the fire, it was like a fever: they broke up all their records. Afterward she burst out crying in a corner, her face to the flames.

Some children, I tell him, kick a package in an empty lot in Buenos Aires. It opens up—and is full of books. Collections of our magazine, banned in the provinces, confiscated in raids, end up in empty lots. You begin to feel that some people greet you in hushed tones or turn their heads away. Even by telephone you can transmit leprosy. Rediscovery of others, now that the tide is rising: who doesn't allow himself to be drowned? Who has the machine not vanquished?

Following the railroad tracks we reach the station. We sit down to smoke a cigarette. On the stones of the platform I discover a lion, a woman combing her hair, a boy with his arms raised as if offering something. The stones have been worn down by the years and footsteps, but it hasn't been possible to erase that. The pointsman who engraved them with a burin is no longer alive. He had become a sculptor due to the long waits. In those days the train passed once a month.

"Yala had its own life," Héctor says. "There used to be people here. There was even a barber. He had St. Vitus' Dance. He was dangerous."

About Europe he tells me little. A phrase in the coat of arms belonging to a house in Andalucía: "To suffer for living." And a film in Paris—the ascetic and very slow life of a mature woman. One night, Jeanne discovers the orgasm. She gets up to wash herself, finds the scissors on the bureau, and plunges them into the throat of the guy.

– 2 –

An iron fist squeezes my neck. I say, to convince myself, that I am not afraid of fear. I am, I say, this desperation that lets me know I'm alive. I'm not going to pay any clown or whore inside me.

I tell Héctor I'm trying to write, to pin down, the little uncertainties that one continually conquers, before the whirlwind of doubt snatches them away—words that are like lion claws or tamarinds in the sand of swirling dunes. Return to the joy of simple things: the light of the candle, the glass of water, the bread I share. Humble dignity, clean world that is worthwhile.

– 3 –

Héctor tells me stories about the old Yala. The girl abandoned by the stranger used to go riding every afternoon. His horse rode at her side, saddled and riderless. She lunched and dined at a table set for two, beside his empty plate. She got old.

We walked along the irrigation ditches, accompanied by the soft murmur. I pulled off a cineraria leaf and squeezed it between my fingers.

"Over there on the comer," Héctor says, "lived a woman who didn't grow; she was also blind. She spent her life seated in a swing. When they swang her, she sang like a bird. It was the only thing she knew how to do."

I talk about Buenos Aires. How many hours has it been since I've heard the wailing of a siren? How much is a man's life worth since that last devaluation? In the countryside, dead bodies and wheat are sown. A name is struck off the list. Where shall the person whose name it is wake up? They gag you, tie up your hands, shove you into the Falcon. You hear the city sounds fade and you say good-bye to what you are thinking because there is a cloth in your mouth:

"No, no. Wait. Not like that. Not forward; he doesn't deserve it. Through the back."

A man becomes aware they are following him. He runs through the streets, rushes into a telephone box. All the numbers he wants are busy or don't answer. Through the window he sees the assassins waiting for him.

Why is it I find it so hard to leave, despite the warnings and threats? Could it be I love this tension from the outside world because it is so like my inner tension?

– 4 –

We return home.

There is a crackling fire in the stove.

We talk about our craft. Celebration of the encounters, mourning for the farewells: Isn't it true that words are able to transport you to where you are no longer? Doesn't one eat and drink, while writing, at tables anywhere? Doesn't one enter women who are yesterday's or tomorrow's? It's nice to know, When you are a stubborn loser of countries, with children and papers spread all over.

Héctor asks me about Haroldo. I tell him we don't know anything. We talk about other prisoners and people who are dead and hunted: about the threats and the banning of words and the links. How long will the hunt continue? How long the treason?

We talk about the magazine. This week the censor rejected an article by Santiago Kovadloff. It was an article against drugs, a denunciation of drugs as masks of fear. He maintained that drugs generate a conservative youth.

The censor decided to keep the original. I told him by phone. When he hung up, Dieguito, his son, saw his worried face. "What's the matter?" he asked, and Santiago replied,

"They don't let us talk. They don't let us say anything."

And Dieguito told him,

"The same thing happens to me with my teacher."

– 5 –

We also talk about the invisible censors.

Could Bergman or Antonioni suspect that inflation has something to do with human noncommunication? The price of the magazine now is forty times the price of the first issue. The cost of a blank page is always more than that of the printed one; and we don't have enough advertising to compensate, due to the sabotage of firms and advertising agencies. For whom do we say the little or nothing they allow us to say? This, Héctor, is looking increasingly like the dialogue of the two silences.

And the threats, aren't they a kind of censure? The printing house has been condemned to being blown up. Our people, those who are not in prison or dead, sleep in strange beds, with one eye open.

– 6 –

We sit down to eat the peppered chicken that Eulalia prepared for us.

Chicha tells the story of the man from Humahuaca who made a pact with the Devil to become invisible.

It does me good to eat at this table. I share the bread and the wine, the memories and the news, like in the old days, when communion gave heart to the believers.

– 7 –

The next morning, Héctor is waiting for me downstairs.

I'm still a bit groggy.

"I listened to the news bulletin," he says. "I have bad news for you, even though you saw it coming. They've found the bodies of Michelini and Gutiérrez Ruiz."

Buenos Aires, May 1976: I Open the Door of the Room Where I'll Sleep Tonight

I'm alone. And I ask myself, does half of me still await me? Where is it? What is it doing in the meantime?

Will the joy arrive wounded? Will its eyes be moist? Answer and mystery of all things: and if we have already passed one another and lost one another without even knowing?

Odd thing: I don't know this half and yet I miss it. I'm nostalgic for a country which doesn't yet exist on a map.

The Old Proverb Says, "Better to Advance and Die than to Stand Still and Die"

— I —

They came in several white cars, the kind the police use. They were armed to the teeth. For a full hour they methodically sacked the home of Gutiérrez Ruiz. They took him away and everything in the house, including the children's magazines. A few yards away stood the armed guards of the embassies of several countries. No one intervened.

Two hours later, they went looking for Zelmar Michelini.

Michelini, who had celebrated his birthday that day, lived in a hotel in the middle of Buenos Aires. They took everything from his place as well. Not even his children's watches were spared. The murderers wore no gloves and their fingerprints were left everywhere. Nobody bothered to look at them.

At the police station, no information on the crime was accepted, despite the fact that Gutiérrez Ruiz had been president of the Uruguayan Chamber of Deputies and Michelini had been a senator for many years. "It would be a waste of paper," the police said.

The next day the Argentine defense minister declared to reporters, without batting an eye, "It was an Uruguayan operation. Whether official or unofficial, I still don't know."

Not long thereafter, in Geneva, the Uruguayan ambassador to the Human Rights Commission said, "Regarding the links between Argentina and Uruguay, of course they exist. We are proud of them. We have a brotherhood based on history and culture."

– 2 –

A few months before, Gutiérrez Ruiz had come to the magazine smiling from ear to ear.

"I've come to give you an invitation," he said. "By the end of the year we'll drink *mate* together in Montevideo."

And Michelini had said,

"What could be worse, *che?* Montevideo or Buenos Aires? Looks like we'll have our choice between torture and a bullet in the neck."

He told me he had been threatened by phone. I didn't ask him why he didn't leave. Like thousands of Uruguayans, Michelini wasn't able to obtain his passport from the authorities. But it wasn't this. I didn't ask him why he didn't leave so he wouldn't ask my why I didn't. The child whistles loudly as he walks past the cemetery gates.

Buenos Aires, June 1976: The Earth Swallows Them

Raimundo Gleizer has disappeared. The usual story. They dragged him out of his house in Buenos Aires, and nothing else is known. He had made unpardonable films.

I had seen him for the last time in February. We went out to dinner with our children, near the sea. Late that night, he told me about his father.

Raimundo's family was from a village on the Polish-Russian border. Every house there had two different flags to hoist and two portraits to hang up, depending on how things went. When the Russian soldiers left, the Polish would come, and so on. It was an area of continual warfare, infinite winter, and endless hunger. The hardened and the quick-witted survived, and in homes, pieces of bread were hidden underneath the floorboards.

World War I was no novelty for anyone in that battered region, but it worsened the worst. Those who didn't die began the day with limp legs and a knot in their stomachs.

In 1918 a shipment of shoes arrived in the region. A ladies' welfare society had sent the shoes from the United States. The hungry from the villages came and tore into each other over the shoes. This was the first time shoes had ever arrived here. No one had ever used shoes in that region. The strongest went home dancing with joy, a box of new shoes under their arms.

Raimundo's father got home, unwrapped the rags around his feet, opened the box and tried on the left shoe. His foot protested, but entered. But his right foot wouldn't go in. Everyone helped push, but there was no way. Then his mother noticed that both shoes were curved in the same direction. He ran back to the distribution center. Everyone had gone.

For months, Raimundo's father walked from village to village, trying to find out.

After a great deal of walking and asking around, he found what he was looking for. In a distant village, beyond the hills, was the man who wore the same size and who had taken the two right shoes. He had placed the shiny new shoes on a shelf. They were the only decoration in his home.

Raimundo's father offered the left shoe.

"Oh no," said the man. "If the Americans sent them that way, that's the way they should be. The Americans know what they are doing. They do things right."

Buenos Aires, June 1976: Street War, Soul War

Sink or join the rest? Erase the others or call them? Solitude is a swindle. Am I going to eat my own vomit, like the camel? What risk does the masturbator run? At the most he can get a stiff wrist.

Reality, others: joy and danger. I beckon the bulls; I resist their onslaught. I know that those fierce horns can smash me.

It is about these things I talk, during long nights, with Santiago Kovadloff. And in lengthy letters to Ernesto Gonzáles Bermejo.

The System

Latin American scientists emigrate, laboratories and universities have no resources, industrial "know-how" is always foreign and costly, but why not recognize a certain creative merit in the development of a technology of terror?

From our lands, those in power make universal contributions to the progress of torture methods, to the techniques used in assassinating people and ideas, to the cultivation of silence, to the multiplication of impotence and the sowing of fear.

I Had Never Heard about Torture

Fifteen years ago, when I worked at the weekly *Marcha,* I interviewed an Algerian student leader. The colonial war had ended during those days.

At first the Algerian didn't want to talk about himself. But as time passed the barriers began to drop and he told me his story—fierce tears of triumph after seven years of struggle. He had been tortured in the Cité Améziane. They had tied him to a metal bed by his wrists and ankles and had administered electric shocks.

"Your heart disappears, your blood disappears, everything sways and disappears."

Later they took him to the submersion tub.

They shot him in the temple with blanks.

Eight officers raped a comrade in front of him.

In those days I did not suspect that torture would become a national custom. I did not know, fifteen years ago, that in the prisons and barracks of my country blackouts would occur because of the excessive use of electricity.

Once in Montevideo, I was eating *fainá* with beer at the corner cafe by the university when I saw René Zavaleta come in.

René was very thin, just arrived from Bolivia, and he talked incessantly.

The Barrientos dictatorship had imprisoned him in Madidi, a military fortress lost in the middle of the jungle. At night, René told me, you could hear the jaguars and the hoards of pigs, which advanced like a cataclysm. The air was always heavy with heat and dark with mosquitoes, and the river made dangerous by sting-rays and piranhas. To enter the hut you had to club the bats to death.

Every day the political prisoners were given a fistful of wheat and half a banana. To get more food you had to stoop down to wash the corporal's feet.

The soldiers, who were also in Madidi as a punishment, spent their time looking up in the sky for a plane that never arrived. René wrote love letters on request. There was no way to get them to girlfriends, but the soldiers liked the letters René wrote and would keep them and every now and then would ask him to read them.

One day two soldiers destroyed each other with their fists. They fought to the death over a cow that had a woman's name.

Then René told me the story of what happened to a friend in the Chaco War.

The System

– 1 –

A famous Latin American playboy doesn't quite make it in his lover's bed. "I drank too much last night," he explains at breakfast. The second night he attributes the failure to exhaustion. The third night he changes lovers. After a week he goes to consult a doctor. A month later, he changes doctors. Some time later, he begins psychoanalysis. Submerged or repressed experiences begin to surface in his consciousness, session after session. And he remembered:

1934. Chaco War. Six Bolivian soldiers wander about on the highland plateau looking for the other troops. They are the survivors of a defeated detachment. They drag themselves over the frozen steppes without seeing a soul or having a bite of food. This man is one of the soldiers.

One afternoon they discover an Indian girl minding a flock of goats. They follow her, knock her down, rape her. Each of them has a turn.

It's the turn of this man, who is the last. As he lies down on the Indian, he notices she is no longer breathing.

The five soldiers stand around him in a circle.

They stick their rifles in his back.

And then, between horror and death, this man chooses horror.

– 2 –

It coincides with a thousand and one stories of torturers.

Who tortures? Five sadists, ten morons, fifteen clinical cases? Respectable heads of families torture. The officers put in their hours of work and then go home to watch television with their children. What is efficient is good, the machine teaches. Torture is efficient: it extracts information, breaks consciences, spreads fear. It is born and it develops the complicity of a black mass. He who doesn't torture will be tortured. The machine accepts neither innocents nor witnesses. Who refuses? Who can keep his hands clean? The little gear vomits the first time. The second time it grits its teeth. The third time it becomes accustomed and does its duty. Time passes and the gear's little wheel speaks the language of the machine: hood, electric prod, submarine, stock, sawhorse.[16] The machine requires discipline. The most talented end up taking a liking to it.

If the torturers are sick, what about the system that makes them necessary?

The System

The torturer is a functionary. The dictator is a functionary. Armed bureaucrats, who lose their jobs if they don't do their tasks efficiently. That, and nothing more than that. They are not extraordinary monsters. We won't grant them that grandeur.

Introduction to Law

He had come from Buenos Aires and was still an outsider in Jujuy, although he had settled in after the years and jobs. One unfortunate day he absent-mindedly paid for a tire with a bad check. He was tried and sentenced. He received a fine. After that his friends crossed over to the other side of the street when they saw him coming. He was invited into no more homes and was never again treated to drinks at bars.

Late one night he went to see the lawyer who had defended him at the trial.

"No, no," he said. "No appeals. I know that nothing can be done. Just leave it. I came to say good-bye and give you a New Year's embrace. A thousand thanks for everything."

In the middle of the night the lawyer woke up with a jump. He nudged his wife awake. "He wished me a Happy New Year and the New Year is two months away."

He got dressed and ran. He didn't find him. The next morning he heard: the man had put a bullet through his head.

Not long thereafter, the judge who had initiated his trial felt a strange pain in his arm. Cancer devoured him in a few months. The prosecutor was killed when a horse kicked him. The man who had replaced him at work lost first his speech, then his sight, then half his body. The car that belonged to the judge's secretary crashed on the road and burned up. A lawyer who had refused to intervene on his behalf was visited by an offended client, who took out his pistol and smashed the lawyer's femoral.

Héctor told me this story in Yala, and I thought about the murderers of Che Guevara.

René Barrientos, the dictator, had given the order to kill him. He ended up enveloped in the flames of his helicopter, a year and a half later. Colonel Zenteno Anaya, commander of the troops that surrounded and trapped Che in Ñancahuázu, transmitted the order. Much later, he got entangled in conspiracies. The dictator of the moment found out. Zenteno Anaya was shot to death in Paris, one spring morning. The Ranger commander Andrés Selich prepared Che's execution. In 1972, Selich was beaten to death by his own functionaries, the Ministry of the Interior's professional torturers. Mario Terán, sergeant, executed the order. He shot the round of machine gun fire into Guevara's body, which was lying in the little schoolhouse in La Higuera. Terán lives in an asylum: he babbles and answers nonsense. Colonel Quintanilla announced the death of Che to the world. He exhibited the body to photographers and journalists. Quintanilla died of three gunshot wounds in Hamburg in 1971.

Buenos Aires, June 1976: Midday

Carlitos called me. He had a couple of free hours.

We met on a corner. We bought a wine we hadn't heard of, Santa Isabel burgundy: we liked the old man in the shop who recommended it, licking his lips.

We went up to a borrowed apartment to eat. It was a one-room apartment. The sheets were strewn on the floor and there was a lovely general disorder. I liked the smell.

"A woman lives here," I said. "And she's a good woman."

"Yes," said Carlitos, "She's quite magical."

He told me that the doctor had said that she couldn't be born. One dawn her mother made a pact with the stars. She was born healthy and the day she came into the world three cows died.

The wine proved to be excellent. Strong, good for savoring on the palate.

We chatted and ate.

Later Carlitos went to work. We arranged to meet on the weekend at Fico's country house.

I still had a little time and I ambled about a bit. I fell asleep on some grass, the autumn sun in my face.

When I woke up, there were two elephants beside me, eating grass.

Written on a Wall, Spoken in the Streets, Sung in the Countryside

— 1 —

Culture didn't end, for us, with the production and consumption of books, paintings, symphonies, films, and plays. It didn't even begin there. We understood culture to be the creation of any meeting space among men, and culture, for us, included all the collective symbols of identity and memory: the testimonies of what we are, the prophecies of the imagination, the denunciations of what prevents us from being. For this reason *Crisis* published, among the poems and stories and drawings, reports on the deceptive teaching of history in the schools or on the wheelings and dealings of the large multinationals that sell automobiles as well as ideology. This is why the magazine denounced a value system that exhaults things and scorns people, and the sinister game of competition and consumption that induces men to use and crush one another. For this reason we were concerned with everything: the sources of the landowners' political power, the oil cartel, the mass media …

— 2 —

We wanted to talk to people, return the word to them: culture is communication or it is nothing. In order for it not to be mute, we thought, a new culture had to begin by not being deaf. We published texts about reality, but also, and above all, texts from reality. Words picked up in the street, in the countryside, in the caves, life histories, popular verses.

The Indians of the Alto Paraná sing of their own agony, surrounded by a civilization which turns them into plantation slaves or kills them in order to seize their land:

"You will watch over the source of the mist engendered by the inspired words. That which I conceived in my solitude, make it watch over your children, the Jakaira of big hearts. Make them call themselves: lord of the mist of the inspired words."

Political prisoners write letters:

"I am going to tell you things about seagulls so you won't keep associating them with sadness."

Anonymous hands write on a wall by the Mar del Plata docks:

"I search for Christ and can't find him.

I search for myself and can't find myself.

But I find my neighbor and together the three of us set out."

From the insane asylum, the poet travels to secret regions:

"I was lying down on the sea. I walked on the waters and called him, 'Lautréamont, Lautréamont,' I cried. And he answered that he loved him. That we would be friends now in the sea, because both of us had suffered on earth."

The children in the schools on the outskirts of Montevideo describe the conquest of America:

"I am coming to civilize. Look at my lovely boat."

"Me no want. Me have house, family and good job."

"But you'll be better off the way I say; then you'll be able to talk like me."

"Stop mucking around and leave me alone."

The factory worker explains his relation to the sun:

"When you go to work it's night and when you leave, the sun is setting. This is why at noon everybody finds five minutes to see the sun in the street, or in a yard at the factory, because you can't see the sun from the shop. The light enters but you never see the sun."

– 3 –

Shortly after the coup d'état, the military government dictated new regulations governing the mass media. According to the new censorship code, it was prohibited to publish street coverage and opinions on any subject given by nonspecialists. The monopoly of power and of the word condemned the common man to silence.

It was the end of *Crisis*. There was little we could do, and we knew it.

The Baker Sings, Happy Because There Is Clay for the Nest

– 1 –

"You're blind," Carlitos said.

He chewed a clover stalk.

We were lying on the grass, away from the others. The white sun barely warmed.

Matías had helped us prepare the charcoal-grilled spareribs. We had eaten and everyone was chatting in groups.

Carlitos had spent his life, he told me, fleeing from his folks. When he discovered his mother, when he was able to see her for the first time, she was a little girl stretched out on her bed and she only said bits of comic or crazy things and she was never going to get up again.

"You're blind," Carlitos said. "Sometimes you guess. Just sometimes."

– 2 –

That night, big ravioli feast. Sarlanga, author of the marvel, told of his misadventures at the Boca field that past Sunday. The crowd had swallowed one of his shoes and he had returned home on the subway with one shoeless foot and a serious face. Achával recalled stories of the old Jauretche, wise and sly, who had been able to recommend a little mourning to that architect of shiny, gaudy clothes.

Every now and then I found myself laughing with and meeting the eyes of a girl called Helena.

I liked her way of eating with gusto.

She had been with us the entire weekend, but it was at dinner that I discovered that Indian face Siqueiros would have liked to paint. I saw abundant light in those greenish eyes, as well as their dry tears, the dignity of her cheekbones, the very womanly mouth marked by the scar: a woman like that should be banned, I thought, with surprise. I did not yet know that it had been a bullet that had grazed her face, but perhaps I already realized that no scrape from death's claws would be able to disfigure her.

Afterward we played cards, and she bet her last cent. She won. Then she pushed everything she had into the middle of the table: and lost. Not a muscle twitched.

We walked together, in the good night chill. The moon, clouded over, let us see the swaying tree tops, slow waves, and the trees were alive, they were accomplices, and the world softly reeled at our feet.

"This is good and clean," I said or she said.

The next night it rained hard in Buenos Aires. We were not together. We didn't sleep, under different roofs, in different neighborhoods, listening to the same rain. And we discovered that we couldn't sleep apart.

– 3 –

The melody found us. The slow, love-lazy melody stretched out and slipped into the air, from room to room, and it found us, languid arrow flight in the air, the melody of "Asa branca": Eric was playing the harmonica for his little son Felipe somewhere in the house and the melody reached us just as I was telling you or you were telling me that it was worthwhile having survived.

My body had grown to find you, after so much walking and stumbling and losing itself. Not the port, the sea: the place where all the rivers end and where the ships and little boats sail.

— 4 —

State of seige, war of extermination, occupied city. We slept in a different bed each time. We were careful, we watched our steps and our words.

But one night, I still don't know how, we found ourselves singing and dancing in the middle of the road, in front of the biggest barracks in Buenos Aires.

Eric, tennis champion who always loses, was spinning around like a top; Acha and Gordo were jumping, arm in arm, and proclaiming the candidacy of Vicente to the government of all empires, monarchies, and republics; Vicente rolled around and jumped and broke a foot shouting how lovely life is. Helena and I celebrated each other like a birthday.

The searchlights found us from the barracks tower. The guard gave the alarm and blinked, "Who are these madmen in disguise singing in the street?"

And he didn't fire.

Dreams

You woke up, restless, in the middle of the night.

"I had a horrible dream. I'll tell you tomorrow, when we're alive. I want it to be tomorrow. Why don't you make today be tomorrow? How I would like it to be tomorrow now."

Will Our Memories Give Us Permission to Be Happy?

There was a moment in which the pain began and from then on it never stopped, it came even though you didn't call it, crow wing shadow repeating into your ear, "No one will be left. No one will be left alive. There are too many mistakes and hopes to be paid for."

The Saracen pulled off the cloth that covered your brother Tin's body, in Córdoba, and while she complained about the heat and too much work she turned his head around so you could see the bullet hole. You didn't notice the tears until you touched your wet skin.

When Rodolfo was gunned down, the first shot hit your mouth. You leaned over his body and you didn't have lips to kiss him.

Afterward …

One by one the loved ones fell, guilty of acting or of thinking or of doubting or of nothing.

That bearded boy with the melancholy gaze arrived at Silvio Frondizi's wake very early, when no one was there. He placed a bright red apple on top of the coffin. You saw him leave the apple and then walk away.

Later you learned that the boy had been Silvio's son. His father had asked him for the apple. They had been eating, at noon, and he had got up to get the apple when the murderers had suddenly broken in.

Buenos Aires, July 1976: Long Trip Without Moving

Rhythm of the lungs of the sleeping city. It's cold outside.

Suddenly, a commotion can be heard through the closed window. You dig your nails into my arm. I don't breathe. We hear blows, curses, and a long human wail.

Afterward, silence.

"Am I heavy?"

Sailor's knot.

Loveliness and slumber more powerful than fear.

When the sun shines in, I blink and stretch with four arms. No one knows who owns this knee, whose elbow or foot this is, whose voice murmurs good morning.

Then the two-headed animal thinks or says or wishes:

"Nothing can happen to people who wake up like this."

The Universe as Seen Through a Keyhole

In those days everything was gigantic. Everything: the stone house on top of the hill, the path of hydrangeas, the men who came home, on the road, when night fell. Wild strawberries grew nearby and the earth was red and looked good enough to bite.

You went down to the city to go to six o'clock mass with Grandmother Deidamia. The yards and the recently paved walks smelled of summer freshness.

Grandmother Deidamia kept in a bureau, wrapped in lace, the umbilical cords of her ten children.

"All the nudity comes from Buenos Aires," she said when you came back from the capital in short sleeves.

Grandmother Deidamia had never had a ray of sun strike her face and she never uncrossed her hands.

Seated in the shade in her rocking chair, hand upon hand, Grandmother would say,

"Here I am, being."

Grandmother Deidamia's hands were transparent, blue-veined, and very long-nailed.

The Universe as Seen Through a Keyhole

You stole a lily from the vase. You took a deep breath of its fragrance. You crossed the yard and the summer heat with slow little steps, the tall flower raised in your fist. The cool tiles in the patio were a joy to your bare feet.

You reached the faucet. To open it, you got up on a bench. The water fell over the flower and your hands and you felt that the water was sliding down all over your body and you closed your eyes, dizzy with so much inexplicable pleasure, and then a century passed.

"My thoughts fell, Mother," you explained later, pointing to the drain on the floor. "They fell down and went in there."

Buenos Aires, July 1976: When Words Cannot Be More Dignified than Silence, It Is Time to Keep Quiet

— I —

We are obliged to submit our galley proofs and manuscript pages to the presidential palace.

"This doesn't go in. Neither does this," they say.

This is how our last meeting with the military went.

Vicente and I had gone.

After discussing the material for an hour, we talked about Haroldo Conti.

"He is an editor of *Crisis*," we said, "and they have kidnapped him. Nothing more has been heard. You tell us he hasn't been detained and the government doesn't have anything to do with it. Why don't you let us publish the news? A ban on this news could give rise to slanted interpretations. You know that abroad there are a lot of people with the wrong idea ..."

"Do you have any complaints against us?" the captain asked. "We have always treated you correctly. We have received you, we have listened to you. That is why we're here and that is our function in the government. But we warn you. This country is at war, and if we were to meet each other on different terrain, the treatment would be quite different."

I touched my companion's knee.

"Let's go, Vicente. It's getting late," I said.

We walked, slowly, through the Plaza de Mayo. We stood for a long time in the middle of the plaza without looking at one another. There was a clear sky and a commotion of people and pigeons. The sun made greenish flashes on the copper cupolas.

We didn't talk.

We entered a cafe, to have a drink, and neither of us dared say, "This means that Haroldo is dead, doesn't it?"

For fear the other would say,

"Yes."

– 2 –

The magazine is finished.

In the morning I get everyone together to talk to them. I want to seem firm and talk hopefully, but sadness escapes through my pores. I explain that neither Fico nor Vicente nor I have made the decision; circumstances have decided. We do not accept humiliation as an epilogue to the beautiful adventure that has brought us together for more than three years. No one makes *Crisis* bow down: we will bury her erect, just as she lived.

– 3 –

I empty my desk drawers, full of my papers and letters. I read, haphazardly, the words of women I loved and men who were my brothers. With my finger I caress the telephone that had brought me friendly voices and threats.

Night has fallen. The compañeros have left a few hours—or months—ago. I hear, I see them; their footsteps and voices, the light that each one gives off and the vapor that remains behind when they leave.

– 4 –

At the newspaper *Época* in Montevideo, it was the same. You walked into that little kid's editorial office and felt embraced even when it was empty.

Ten years have passed—or an instant. How many centuries make up this moment I'm now living? How many airs form the air I breath? Times gone by, airs blown past: years and air kept in me and from me, multiplied when I sit down and put on my magician's cape or captain's hat or clown's nose and I grip the pen and write. I write, that is, prophesy, navigate, beckon. Coming?

Tattered backdrop, ship, makeshift circus. We all worked out of faith, of which there was an excess: no one got paid. Every now and then a girl would drop by to give us liver pills or shots of vitamins. We were young and eager to do things and speak out: we were happy and stubborn, contagious.

Once in a while the government would close us down and dawn would find us at the police station. We received the news with more relief than indignation. Every day we didn't publish was a day to get money together so we could come out the next. We would go to the police headquarters with Andrés Cultelli and Manrique Salbarrey and at the door we would say good-bye just in case.

Will we be out today? We never knew. Midnight passed and the agencies had removed the teletypes, for lack of payment; they had cut off our telephone, and our only radio fell and broke. The typewriters didn't have ribbons and at 2:00 a.m. we went out in search of rolls of newsprint. All we would have to do was to go out on the balcony and wait for a love drama to unfold on the street corner, but we didn't have film for our cameras either. We even had a fire that wrecked our shop machinery. I don't know how *Época* made it to the streets every morning. Proof of the existence of God or the magic of solidarity?

We were too young to regret our joy. At 3:00 a.m., when the job was done, we opened up a space between the editorial desks and played soccer with some paper wadded into a ball. Sometimes the referee could be bought off for a plate of beans or a black tobacco cigarette, and then the fists flew until the shop sent up the first copy of the paper: ink-smelling, finger-stained, just born from the mouth of the press. That was a birth. Afterward we walked arm in arm to the boulevard to wait for the sun. That was a ritual.

Who could forget those lovely fellows? Don't I recognize that pulse, that sound, in my people now? Is it good for anything, my memory? We have tried to break the lie-machine ... Memory. My poison, my food.

"The Tree Flies," Says the Poet, "In the Bird that Leaves It."

– 1 –

One afternoon in Montevideo, in the summer of 1960 or 1961, I discovered I could no longer stand that guy who put on a tie and shiny jacket at the proper time and counted bills and gave out change and good-mornings with clenched teeth. I shut the cash box, and made out the balance sheet, signed it and told the bank manager,

"I'm leaving."

And he said,

"It's not time yet."

And I told him,

"I'm going for good."

And I went to Buenos Aires for the first time.

I was twenty years old. I knew just a few people in Buenos Aires, but I thought I could manage.

At first Babylonia treated me quite badly. I felt lonely and persecuted by the crowds and the heat and the lack of money.

I worked for a short time at the magazine *Che,* until one morning I arrived at the editorial offices with Chiquita Constenla and Pablo Giussani and we found the building surrounded by police. It was during the days of the railroad strike. The workers were burning railroad cars and the magazine didn't think this was so bad. The soldiers broke down the door.

For a week I didn't see anyone. I was buried in a "hotel/ rooming house," as they call it there, where they didn't request identification papers or ask questions. I rolled around in my bed day and night, a puddle of perspiration and sadness, kept awake by the yells and the doors slammed and the couples who groaned through the walls.

– 2 –

An image remained with me from that first period in Buenos Aires which I'm not sure was real or dreamed up some awful night: the crowds pressed together at a subway station, sticky air, a feeling of suffocation, and the subway wasn't coming. A half hour passed, perhaps more, and the news got around that a girl had thrown herself onto the tracks at the station just before ours. At first there were silences, remarks in low, funeral-like voices. "Poor little thing, poor little thing," they said. But the train still didn't come and it was getting late for work and then people began stamping nervously and saying, "But why couldn't she have thrown herself across another train line? Why did it have to be just this one?"

I crossed the river and vowed never to return. But I returned, many times. And in early 1973 Fico Vogelius placed me in charge of a magazine that was to be called *Crisis.*

– 3 –

In mid-1976 there was nothing to do but leave. It wasn't easy. The city which I had hated in earlier days had treated me to dangers, jubilation, loves. How many people are shaded by the magnolias of Plaza Francia? What multitudes filled my mind when I passed the "Ramos," the "Ciervo," or the "Bachín"?

In the "Ramos" at midday, Manolo would toss peanuts onto the wood floors. Some pigeon would leave the sunlight on the sidewalk and come in to eat. With Manolo, the waiter of the "Ramos," we would watch the people pass by on the avenue.

"How are you doing?"

"The same as the country."

"Surviving?"

"Who, me?"

"The country, I mean."

"Lying, poor thing."

– 4 –

On the eve of our departure, Helena and I ate with Achával and Carlitos Domínguez. Acha raised his glass of wine and toasted,

"To better times," he said. "We've seen the worst."

Achával lived far away, more than an hour from Buenos Aires. He didn't want to stay out late in the city because it was sad riding the trains alone at daybreak.

Every day at nine in the morning Acha got on the train to go to work. He always got on the same car and sat in the same seat.

In front of him rode a woman. Every day, at 9:25, that woman would get off for a minute at a station—always the same one where a man stood waiting—always in the same place. The woman and the man would embrace and kiss until the whistle blew. Then she would break away and return to the train.

That woman sat in front of him, but Acha never heard her voice.

One morning she didn't come and, at 9:25, Acha saw, through the window, the man waiting on the platform. She never came again. After a week, the man disappeared as well.

Street War, Soul War

Suddenly you are under foreign skies and in lands where people speak and feel differently and even your memory doesn't have people to share nor places to recognize yourself in. You have to fight with all you have to earn your living and your sleep and you feel as if you were crippled, with so much missing.

You're tempted to whine, the viscous domain of nostalgia and death, and you run the risk of living with your head turned backward, a living death, which is one way to prove that a system which scorns the living is right. Ever since we were children, and in the hypocrisy of funerals, we have been taught that death is something that improves people.

The Winds and the Years

– I –

The Dutchman stuck his head out from among the dead ships. From under his cap, which had once been blue, hung very white locks of hair. He didn't greet me, but looked at me unblinkingly with his immense transparent eyes set in his long face.

I sat down nearby, in the remains of a hull, while he cut up masts and spars with a saw, pliers, and patience.

The Dutchman had a running battle with the seagulls. He said they stole food from him. It was hard for him to believe I was there just out of pleasure. The dock was some ten or twelve blocks from home and it was good to walk down there, on sunny afternoons, and find the sea. Sometimes the Dutchman let me help him. I would jump from boat to boat, rescuing rust-coated anchors, broken tillers, and ropes that smelled of tar.

He worked in silence. On afternoons when he was in a good mood he told stories of shipwrecks and mutinies and whale-hunting in the southern seas.

– 2 –

When they invited me to Cuba in 1970 as a judge for the Casa de las Americas contest, I went down to the docks to say good-bye.

"I've been in La Habana," he said. "In those days I was young and had a white suit. I worked on a large ship. I liked that port and I stayed there. One morning at breakfast I read an ad in the paper. A French lady wanted to begin a relationship with a well-educated, good-looking young man. I took a bath, shaved, and put on shoes that matched my suit. The house was near the cathedral. I went up the stairs and knocked with my cane. There was a big doorknocker, but I had a cane. Then the door opened. The Frenchwoman was completely naked. I stood there, wide-mouthed. And I asked her, 'Madame ou mademoiselle?'"

We laughed.

"It's been a long time since then," said the Dutchman. "And now I want to ask you to do something for me."

– 3 –

As soon as I reached Cuba I went to the La Habana fortress. I couldn't get in. It was a military zone. I talked with everyone and couldn't get permission.

When I returned to Montevideo, I walked to the dock and stood for a long while, looking at the Dutchman work. I smoked two or three cigarettes. The refinery flame rose up at the foot of the mountain. The Dutchman didn't question me. I told him that in La Habana I had seen, intact, as if newly engraved in the stone wall of the fortress, the words of love he had written there, in 1920, with a nail.

Chronicle of Gran Tierra

– 1 –

The first time I went to Cuba was in mid-1964. It was during the height of the total blockade: the passage of people and things was prevented.

We went to Lima and then to Mexico. From Mexico to Windsor and Montreal. We had a five-day wait in Montreal—the "belle province" on automobile plates; "private property" on the lakeside signs and from there to Paris and from Paris on to Madrid.

We landed in Madrid in the morning. We just needed to stop over in Oceania. But in Madrid we learned that the plane would leave for La Habana that night.

Reina and I decided to visit the Prado Museum. Reina, a fellow member of the delegation to the anniversary of the Moncada, was a fat and wise grandmother, teacher of several generations, with an untiring spark of intelligence in her eyes and her own very special way of sighing. We had become pals on the long trip.

Thanks to the blockade I had an opportunity, that afternoon, I had always hoped for: to see El Greco's knights exactly as they had been painted by his hand, Velázquez' light unfalsified by reproductions, and above all, the black painting of Goya, the monsters that his soul had given birth to and that had stayed with him, in the Quinta del Sol, to the end of his days.

We reached the museum doors. The Paseo del Prado was marvelous that clean summer noon.

"Shall we have a cup of coffee before going in?"

There were tables on the sidewalks. We ordered coffee and dry sherry.

Reina wasn't one to hold grudges, but she yawned recalling her first marriage. She had lived a number of years as a traditional mother and lady of the house. One night, at a party, she had been introduced to a man. She gave him her hand and he squeezed it and held on to it, and she felt, for the first time, a strange electricity, and suddenly discovered that her body, until that instant, had been mute and music-less. They didn't say a word to one another. Reina never saw him again. She could remember neither the name nor the face of this man who had changed her life.

We ordered more coffee and sherry.

Reina talked about her loves and I never noticed the hours flying by. When we remembered, it was too late. We didn't go to the Prado Museum. I forgot that a Prado Museum existed.

Then we boarded the plane, laughing to death.

– 2 –

When I returned to Cuba six years later, the revolution was going through its most difficult period. The 10-million-ton sugarcane harvest had failed. The concentrated effort on sugarcane production had left the national economy askew. At last the children had milk and shoes, but in the dining halls at workplaces meat was a miracle and some fruits and vegetables existed only in memory.

In grave tones, Fidel Castro read the dramatic statistics to the multitude. "Here are the secrets of the Cuban economy," he said.

"Yes, *señores imperialistas!*" he said. "It is very difficult to construct socialism!"

The revolution had toppled the high walls. Now shelter, clothes, and food, the alphabet and the doctor, the freedom of choice belonged to everyone. But hadn't the country been schooled for centuries in impotence and resignation? With what legs could production catch up to consumption? Could Cuba run, if it was just learning how to stand on its own feet?

Fidel spoke, as night fell on the immense plaza, of the tensions and the difficulties. And, at more length, he spoke about the errors. He analyzed the vices of disorganization, the bureaucratic deviations, the mistakes that had been made. He admitted to his own inexperience, which had sometimes led him to act unrealistically, and he said that there were some who thought that he was where he was because he liked power and glory.

"I have given this revolution the best years of my life," he said.

And with a scowl he asked,

"What does glory mean? Why, all the glories in the world fit in just one grain of corn!"

He explained that when the revolution is real, it works for the times and people to come. The revolution's pulse was too fast and it was breathless, in the face of the persecution and the blockade and the threat.

"The enemy says that in Cuba we have difficulties," said Fidel.

The faces and fists of the crowd, which listened in silence, tightened.

"And the enemy is right about that."

"The enemy says that in Cuba there is discontent," he added. "And the enemy is also right about that."

"But there is one thing the enemy is mistaken about!"

And then he stated that the past would not return; in a thunderous voice he stated that Cuba would never return to the hell of the colonial plantation and the whorehouse for foreigners, and the multitude responded with an earthshaking roar.

That night the teletypes went crazy announcing the imminent fall of Fidel Castro. Trained in lying, some reporters couldn't understand the courage of the truth. Fidel Castro's sincerity that night had been the measure of the greatness and the strength of the revolution.

I had the luck to have been there and I do not forget it.

– 3 –

In his house in La Habana, Bola de Nieve besieged me with questions about Montevideo and Buenos Aires.[17] He wanted to know all about the lives of people and about places he had known and loved thirty or forty years ago. After a while I realized it didn't make sense to keep saying, "It doesn't exist anymore," or "It was forgotten." He understood as well, I think, because he began to talk about Cuba, about what he called "Yoruba-Marxism-Leninism"; the invincible synthesis of African magic and the science of whites, and he spent hours telling jokes about the high society that had paid him to sing in the old days: "Rosalía Abreu had two orangutans. She dressed them in overalls. One served her breakfast and the other made love to her."

He showed me the paintings of Amalia Peláez, who had been his friend.

"She died of stupidity," he said. "At seventy-one she was still a virgin. She had never had a lover—male or female or anything."

He confessed his terror of live roosters and loose monkeys.

He say down at the piano, and sang "Drume negrita." Afterward he sang "Ay, Mama Inés," and the cry of the peanut vendor. His voice was quite wasted away but the piano helped lift it up every time it fell.

At one point he interrupted his song and stopped with his hands in the air. He turned around to me and said in astonishment,

"The piano believes me. It believes everything, every little thing."

– 4 –

When the Casa de las Américas work was over, Sergio Chaple proposed we travel to Gran Tierra.

We flew over the jungle in a nutshell, and landed at the end of the country. On the horizon shone the blue mountains of Haiti.

"No, no," Magüito said. "This isn't where Cuba ends. This is where it begins."

The land at the end of Maisí is dry, although it lies on the edge of the sea. Droughts lay waste to vegetable and bean crops. The four winds cross in Maisí, blowing the clouds away and driving off the rains.

Magüito took us to his home for coffee.

As we entered we woke up a sow sleeping in the doorway. She got furious. We sipped coffee surrounded by children, pigs, goats, and chickens. On the wall was Saint Barbara, flanked by two Buddhas and a Heart of Christ.

There were many lit candles. Magüito had lost a granddaughter the week before.

"The time had come. She had lost her color; she had become a cotton flower. Nothing is worth anything when the time has come. We are all here for a time. And sometimes before that time they light the candles for you, like they did for me thirty-seven years ago and he won't last 'til tomorrow, they say, and then you stand up."

Through the wide-open door we could see the fishermen pass by. They came from the sea, with porgies and Caribbean perch hanging on rods, already cleaned and salted, ready to dry. The dust from the road rose in clouds behind them.

When the first helicopter arrived in this region, the people fled, panic-stricken. Until the triumph of the revolution, the seriously ill were carried on cots through the jungle, and they died before reaching Baracoa. But no one was surprised when our little plane arrived at the new airport, and it had been some time since the bearded ones had built the first hospital in Los Llanos.

"Men with blood in their veins can't stand abuses," Magüito said. "It's my defect. If I have enemies, they are hidden. I was a *son* and *danzón* dancer, drinker, and party-goer, a good friend. From here on up, everyone knows me."

And he warned us,

"We're not mean-tempered here. We keep our guard up but we don't cut each other up. The people up there, in Gran Tierra, they're worse than the blue mosquito."

– 5 –

On the road, the brilliance hurt our eyes. The wind, which blew low and in whirlwinds, covered people and things with masks of reddish dust.

The local people hated bats. At night, bats would leave the caves and fall on the coffee. They would bite the grain, sucking out the honey. The grains would dry and fall off.

– 6 –

On the cliffs overlooking the sea, lay Patana Arriba. Below, facing the reefs, Patana Abajo. Everyone's name was Mosqueda.

"Between children and grandchildren," said don Cecilio, "I was counting the other night, and there were approximately three hundred. There's no woman in the house anymore. I'm almost eighty-seven. I used to raise goats, cattle, and hogs, down below. Here it looks like I'm having luck with coffee. Have I fished? Fished or sinned?[18] Do I still remember?"

He winked an eye.

"Something is left. In memory and impulse."

And he added, with a smile that revealed his toothless gums,

"There's a reason Mosqueda is the reigning name, the one that multiplies most."

We were thirsty. Don Cecilio Mosqueda jumped up from the rocking chair.

"I'll go up," he said.

One of his grandchildren, or great grandchildren, Braulio, grabbed his arm and sat him down.

Braulio climbed up the high trunk, gripping with his feet. He balanced on the branches, machete in hand. A shower of coconuts fell to the ground.

Don Cecilio was curious about the tape recorder. I showed him how it worked.

"That gadget is really scientific," he said, "because it keeps the voice of the dead alive."

He scratched his chin. Pointing to the recorder with his index finger he said, "I want you to put this in there." And he spoke as he rocked, his eyes closed.

Braulio was the head of the patriarch's snail gatherers. The brigades of grandchildren and great grandchildren took turns sleeping. At the slightest carelessness, don Cecilio would escape from them on horseback and in one sprint would gallop through the jungle and reach Baracoa by daybreak, where he would throw compliments at the girl he was crazy about, or he would walk up the hills to Montecristo, which was quite a distance, to serenade the other girl who gave him sleepless nights.

Don Cecilio didn't object to the revolution.

"People used to live in a very isolated way, rebellious-like," he explained. "Now they exchange culture."

He had discovered the radio. The household parrot had learned a Beatles song and don Cecilio had heard about certain things that occurred in La Habana.

"I don't like the beach. I almost never go. But I have heard that in La Habana there is something called the 'bikini,' that women air all their little hairs. And something happens then. That only you should see what belongs to your woman. Aren't you the one who assists her? I'm a man who likes order, and it's on the beach and at dances where the foolishness begins. So how did my woman dress? Over her head, *chico*, and she got undressed over her feet."

Divorce also concerned him. He had heard that there were a lot of divorces, and that that isn't taken seriously.

"But don Cecilio," interrupted Sergio. "Isn't it true that you had over forty women?"

"Forty-nine," don Cecilio admitted. "But I never got married. If you get married you're lost."

Afterward we wanted to get him to talk, but don Cecilio wasn't giving away anything about the treasure. Everyone around knew he had a treasure buried in a cave.

– 7 –

We headed toward a little town called La Máquina.

The truck picked the people up. Everyone was going to the assembly.

"Plácido, come on, let's go. You're not getting away, Plácido."

"They didn't tell me about it!"

They waited for the truck fresh from baths, in ironed clothes, the old ladies carrying colored parasols, the girls in party dresses, the men crooked in their new shoes. On the truck, the dust immediately covered skin and clothes and you had to close your eyes: they recognized each other by their voices.

"Don Cecilio? He's an old man of the ancient kind from before. He's more than one hundred years old."

"He's going to die without saying where he has the treasure. Nobody is going to pray for him."

"What do you say, Ormidia?"

"That his soul won't rest, Iraida."

"And how could it rest? With so much sin and the tremendous load of dirt it'll have on top of it."

"Do I have a lot of dirt on me?"

"I can't see you, Urbino."

"Just what's necessary and no more."

"Nobody asked you, Arcónida."

The truck bounced from hole to hole. The branches whipped our faces and colored snails fell off the trees. Between bump and bump I stuffed handfuls of them into my pockets.

"Don't be afraid, the world isn't ending."

"The world is just beginning, Urbino."

Several children, two dogs, and a parrot were also aboard. Everyone hung on as best they could. I clung to a water pipe.

Every now and then the motor would stop and we would have to get out to push.

"I'm chosen," said Urbino. "Good for everything except for going."

We were still far away from our destination when we had a flat tire.

"There's no way to fix it. It died."

And the procession set out on the road.

The rest of the way was uphill.

Men and women, children and creatures sang as they climbed the mountain.

I tuned my voice. "See? What a chest I have!"

They were sticky from sweat and dust and they happily waged battle against the summer sun, the three o'clock sun, which punished pitilessly.

"El día que yo me muera
¿quién se acordará de mi?
Solamente la tinaja
Por el agua que bebí."

["The day I die
Who will remember me?
Just the water jug
For the water I drank."]

Urbino, who was lame, held on to my shirt as he walked.

"I sing what I know and I don't owe anything to or fear the world," he said. "Do you know this rhythm? It's ours. It's called *nengón*. It's a Patana rhythm, but Patana Abajo. It's played with maracas. And with a guitar, one with four wire strings, which is also our invention. In the deserted land of Patana, we have to invent."

The tops of the palm trees were shimmering white. I thought an ice-cold beer would be like a blood transfusion.

"Ten thousand things are happening here that Fidel doesn't even know about," Urbino said. "You tell them in La Habana to send me the *habilites* they promised me. Don't forget, eh?"

He had bought an electric motor for his carpentry shop. He had consulted beforehand and had been told to go ahead and buy it, so he could bring electric light to the townspeople as well as make furniture for everyone. But the motor had never worked and the townsfolk had scoffed.

"Those empty pieces of iron," they told him. "That motor is a big gyp, Urbino. They took you for a ride."

"Without the motor, we're still in the dark. Do you understand? You tell them to send them to me. The *habilites*, to habilitate the motor, which is all the stuff that comes inside."

The hill was behind us now and we could see the first little wooden houses. Some wild bulls crossed the road and fled. From the banana plants hung swollen violet buds, ready to burst open. I stopped to wait for an old lady who was dragging her long green dress.

"When I was young I flew," she said. "Not now."

The whole of Gran Tierra was in assembly. No one complained and the songs continued until the floor was taken by a blond peasant with high cheekbones and hard features, who talked about organization and tasks. He was the region's top technician in mechanized agriculture.

Afterward he invited Sergio and me to eat fried plantains.

He had learned to read and write at the age of twenty-five.

– 8 –

We gathered quite a few colored snails. We emptied them with a needle, one by one, and let them dry in the sun. I was amazed by these minuscule marvels, the *polimitas,* with their endless variety of color and design. They lived on tree trunks and under the broad banana plant leaves. Every snail painted its house better than Picasso or Miró.

In the Patanas I had been given a snail that was hard to find. It was called *Ermitaño* [hermit]. It was very difficult to empty it. The snail was hidden way back at the end of the mother-of-pearl corkscrew; even when dead it wouldn't come out. It gave off a disgusting smell, but it was a rare beauty. The shell, with copper-colored streaks and the shape of a Malaysian dagger, didn't seem made to spin chubbily like a top, but to unfold and fly.

– 9 –

Aurelio told us that they had warned him, "Don't go to Patana, because they burn people there and bury them on the sly. They also work damned fast, the Pataneros."

We were in Asunción. During the day, Aurelio had accompanied us everywhere. He didn't sleep at night. He stayed with us until someone, down below, whistled three times. Aurelio jumped out the window and was lost in the foliage. After a while he returned. He lay in his bed, smoking.

"You're hexed, Aurelio," Sergio told him.

He knocked at our door sometime during the night.

He was afraid of nightmares. He would concentrate on a point within a circle and when he managed to sleep a giant nail would come and bury itself in his chest, or an enormous magnet he couldn't shake free of, or an iron piston that squeezed him against the wall and broke a vertebra.

Aurelio was in the army, seventh year, artillery.

"They want to discharge me. I asked them to wait. I'm hanging on there because I like it."

He had tried to go to Venezuela to fight. He and other boys on scholarships had been on their way when they were caught. Fidel talked to them. He said they were too young; they'd do better to study.

"When I was flying to Gran Tierra, in the little plane, I imagined I had a mission. I was a courier, in Venezuela or Bolivia. At the airport, the police were waiting for me. I escaped on the roof of a train."

– 10 –

We ran into Aurelio quite early, on the edge of town. He had a pitchfork in one hand and a machete in the other. He told us he was returning from killing snakes. He hunted for them among the rocks and weeds and cut off their heads or broke their bones.

He showed us the machete, which had belonged to his father.

"One time in Camagüey, Matías, the Haitian, took it away from me. He didn't yank it away or anything. They know how it's done. 'Look out, I'm going to get you,' I said, and I raised the machete. Old Matías didn't even touch me. He crossed his arms, uncrossed them, and then I don't know, it was like I was blinded, and he already had the machete, tied by the handle."

In the cafeteria we found a crowd of girls.

"What happened to the shell?" one asked. "Do you have it, brown-hair?"

Aurelio blushed.

Sergio whispered advice,

"That thin one is juicy."

The girls were having a discussion.

"Colors were made for different tastes."

"The way people dress has nothing to do with it. It doesn't affect the way people are."

"Oh no? The best wedding dress is bare skin."

"You marry just once and forever."

"And if the man turns out to be a ninny? You have to live with him, to know."

"Tell us Narda. Where was that person from who said that to fall in love ..."

"Well, I have higher moral standards than the Turquino peak."[19]

"Oh, my god. We have such old-fashioned ways here I can't stand them anymore."

This thin girl's name was Bismania—a name she had chosen when her own had ceased to please her.

– II –

Nearby a construction brigade was building walls. We offered to lend a hand.

"I don't like any of those girls," Aurelio said.

We worked until nightfall. The three of us got white from the lime and hard from the cement.

Aurelio confessed he had come to Gran Tierra in pursuit of a girl. Now she had been locked up. She was the one who had sent the messengers who whistled in the night under the window. This is how she met with Aurelio, for an instant, among the trees.

But that night no one whistled and Aurelio didn't knock on the door.

We didn't see him the next day.

When we asked about him, he was already flying back to La Habana.

"He wanted to steal the *guajira* [peasant girl]," they told us. "His father sent for him."

Aurelio's father wore three stripes on his first captain's collar. (Aurelio was six and it was four days after Fulgencio Batista had fled in a plane. Aurelio saw an enormous man coming down the Baracoa beach. He had a beard that reached his chest and wore an olive-colored uniform.

"See," his mother told him, "That's your father." Aurelio ran along the beach. The immense man lifted him up and hugged him.

"Don't cry," he said. "Don't cry.")

News

From Uruguay.

A girl from Salto died while being tortured. Another prisoner committed suicide.

The prisoner had been in the Libertad jail for three years. One day he acted up or looked suspicious or some guard got up on the wrong side of the bed. The prisoner was sent to the punishment cell. There they call it "the island": incommunicado, hungry, asphyxiated in the "island," the prisoners cut their veins or went crazy. This man spent a month in the punishment cell. Then he hanged himself.

The news is routine, but one detail jumps out at me. The prisoner's name was José Artigas.

Street War, Soul War

Will we be capable of learning humility and patience?

I am the world, but very small. A man's time is not history's time, although, admittedly, we would like it to be.

The System

I recall something Miguel Littín told me five or six years ago. He had just filmed *La tierra prometida* in the Ranquil valley, a poor region of Chile.

The local peasants were "extras" in the scenes where there were masses. Some of them played themselves. Others played soldiers. The soldiers invaded the valley, and with bloodshed and fire, threw the peasants off the land. The film was the chronicle of the massacre.

The problems began on the third day. The peasants who wore uniforms, rode horseback, and shot blanks had become arbitrary, bossy, and violent. After each day of filming, they would harass the other peasants.

Street War, Soul War

How many times have I been a dictator? How many times an inquisitioner, a censor, a jailer? How many times have I forbidden those I most loved freedom and speech? How many people have I felt I owned? How many people have I sentenced because they committed the crime of not being me? Is it not more repugnant to hold people as private property than things? How many people have I used, I who thought myself so marginal to the consumer society? Have I not desired or celebrated, secretly, the defeat of others, I who aloud claimed no interest in success? Who fails to reproduce, within himself, the world that makes him? Who is free from confusing his brother with a rival and the woman he loves with his own shadow?

Street War, Soul War

Does writing have any meaning? The question lies heavily in my hand.

Custom houses for words, incinerations of words, cemeteries for words are organized. So we will resign ourselves to live a life that is not ours, they force us to recognize an alien memory as our own. Masked reality, history as told by the winners: perhaps writing is no more than an attempt to save, in times of infamy, the voices that will testify to the fact that we were here and this is how we were. A way of saving for those we do not yet know, as Espriu had wanted, "the name of each thing." How can those who don't know where they come from find out where they're going?

Introduction to Art History

I dine with Nicole and Adoum.

Nicole talks about a sculptor she knows, a man of much talent and fame. The sculptor works in an enormous workshop, surrounded by children. All the neighborhood children are his friends.

One fine day the mayor's office commissioned him to make a huge horse for the city plaza. A truck brought a gigantic block of granite to the shop. The sculptor began to work on it, standing on a ladder, hammering and chiseling away. The children watched him work.

Then the children went away to the mountains or the seaside on vacation.

When they returned, the sculptor showed them the finished horse.

And one of the children asked him, wide-eyed,

"But ... how did you know that inside the stone there was a horse?"

News

From Argentina.

Luis Sabini is safe. He was able to leave the country. He had disappeared at the end of 1975 and a month later we knew they had imprisoned him.

There is no trace of Haroldo Conti. They went to Juan Gelman's house in Buenos Aires looking for him. Since he wasn't there, they took his children. His daughter reappeared a few days later. Nothing is known about his son. The police say they don't have him; the armed forces say the same thing. Juan was going to be a grandfather. His pregnant daughter-in-law also disappeared. Cacho Paoletti, who sent us texts from La Rioja, was tortured and is still in prison. Other writers published in the magazine: Paco Urondo, shot down, a while ago, in Mendoza; Antonio Di Benedetto, in jail; Rodolfo Walsh, disappeared. On the eve of his kidnapping, Rodolfo sent a letter denouncing the fact that today the "Triple A" is the three armed forces: "The very source of terror which has lost its course and can only babble the discourse of death."

Dreams

You wanted a light and the matches wouldn't light. Not one match would light. All the matches were headless or wet.

Calella de la Costa, June 1977: To Invent the World Each Day

We chat, we eat, we smoke, we walk, we work together, ways of making love without entering each other, and our bodies call each other as the day travels toward the night.

We hear the last train pass. Church bells. It's midnight.

Our own little train slips and flies, travels along through airs and worlds, and afterward morning comes and the aroma announces tasty, steamy, freshly made coffee. Your face radiates a clean light and your body smells of love juices.

The day begins.

We count the hours that separate us from the night to come. Then we will make love, the sorrowcide.

If You Listen Closely, All of Us Make Just One Melody

Crossing the fern-filled field, I reach a river bank.

This is a morning of fresh sunlight. A soft breeze blows. From the chimney of the stone house the smoke flows and curls. Ducks float on the water. A white sail slips between the trees.

My body has, this morning, the same rhythm as the breeze, the smoke, the ducks, and the sail.

Street War, Soul War

I pursue the enemy voice that has ordered me to be sad. At times I feel that joy is a crime of high treason, and I am guilty of the privilege of being alive and free.

Then it helps me to remember what Chief Huillca said in Peru, speaking before the ruins. "They came here. They even smashed the rocks. They wanted to make us disappear. But they have not been able to, because we are alive, and that is the main thing." And I think that Huillca was right. To be alive: a small victory. To be alive, that is: to be capable of joy, despite the good-byes and the crimes, so that exile will be a testimony to another, possible country.

The task ahead—building our country—cannot be accomplished with bricks of shit. Will we be of any use if, when we return, we are broken?

Joy takes more courage than grief. In the end, we are accustomed to grief.

Calella de la Costa, July 1977: The Market

The fat plum, with its pure juice that drowns you in sweetness, should be eaten, you taught me, with closed eyes. The beet plum, with its tight, red pulp, is looked at when eaten.

You like to caress the peach and to strip it with a knife, and you prefer dull-colored apples so you can bring out the shine with your hands.

Lemons inspire your respect and oranges make you laugh. There's nothing nicer than mountains of radishes and nothing more ridiculous than pineapples, with their medieval warrior's armor.

Tomatoes and peppers seem born to display themselves belly to the sun in baskets, sensually bright and lazy, but tomatoes really begin their lives when mixed with oregano, salt, and oil, and peppers don't find their fate until the heat from the oven leaves them bright red and our mouths eagerly devour them.

The spices in the market are a world apart. They are minuscule and powerful. Meats unfailingly get excited and give off juices when penetrated by spices. We are always aware that if it had not been for spices we would not have been born in America and magic would have been lacking at our tables and in our dreams. After all, it was they who spurred on Christopher Columbus and Sinbad the Sailor.

The little bay leaves have a lovely way of breaking in your hand before failing softly onto the roast meat or ravioli. You're very fond of rosemary and verbena, nutmeg, basil, and cinnamon, but you'll never know if it's because of the smells, the tastes, or the names. Parsley, the spice of the poor, has advantages over all others: it's the only one that reaches your plate green and alive and wet with fresh little drops.

While the Ceremony Lasts We Are, With Her,a Little Bit Sacred

I open the bottle of wine. In Buenos Aires, the black, pot-bellied bottle of "San Felipe." Here, "Sangre de Toro" from the Torres vineyards.

I serve the wine and we let it sit in our glasses for a while. We sniff it and celebrate the color, luminous in the candlelight.

Legs search for each other and knot under the table.

The glasses kiss. The wine is pleased by our happiness. The good wine, which disdains the drunk and gets bitter in the mouths of those who don't deserve it.

The sauce simmers and bubbles in the stew-pot, slow tides of thick, reddish, steaming sauce: we eat slowly, savoring ourselves, talking unhurriedly.

To eat alone is a bodily necessity. With you, it is a mass and a laugh.

News

From Uruguay.

They have burned the collections and the archives of *Marcha.*

Shutting it down was not enough for them.

Marcha had been alive thirty-five years. Every week it demonstrated, by just existing, that it is possible to not sell oneself.

Carlos Quijano, who always headed it, is in Mexico. He just escaped.

Marcha no longer existed and Quijano insisted on remaining, as if at a wake. He would come to the editorial offices at the usual time and sit at his desk, and there he remained until the night, faithful ghost in the empty castle: he opened the few letters that still arrived and answered the telephone when it rang by mistake.

The System

Extermination plan: destroy the grass, pull up every last little living thing by the roots, sprinkle the earth with salt. Afterward, kill all memory of the grass. To colonize consciences, suppress them; to suppress them, empty them of the past. Wipe out all testimony to the fact that in this land there ever existed anything other than silence, jails, and tombs.

It is forbidden to remember.

Prisoners are organized into work gangs. At night they are forced to whitewash the phrases of protest that in other times covered the walls of the city.

The steady pelting of rain on the walls begins to dissolve the white paint. And little by little the stubborn words reappear.

News

From Argentina.

At 5:00 p.m., purification by fire. In the barracks yard of the Fourteenth Regiment of Córdoba, the Third Army Command "proceeds to incinerate this pernicious documentation, in defense of our most traditional spiritual heritage, synthesized in God, Fatherland, and Home." The billowing clouds of smoke can be seen from afar.

Translator's Notes

1. This is a reference to a 1572 massacre of Protestant leaders in Paris.
2. The Broad Front (Frente Amplio) was a coalition of Socialists, Communists, Christian Democrats, and elements of Argentina's traditional parties which won 20 percent of the presidential vote in the November 1971 elections. Its candidate, General Liber Seregni, was arrested by the military in July 1973. and remains imprisoned today.
3. Héctor Cámpora was elected president of Argentina in March 1973 as a candidate of the Peronist party and a stand-in for Juan Perón, who was not permitted to run. He resigned in July, paving the way for Perón's own election.
4. Raúl Sendic was a founder of the National Liberation Movement (Tupamaros) in Uruguay. He was taken prisoner in a battle with police in September 1972.
5. Luis Britto is a Venezuelan writer and journalist.
6. In his last speech to the Chilean people, shortly before the air force bombed the Presidential Palace, Allende spoke of his belief that "sooner, rather than later, the grand avenues would open" for those who will build a better society.
7. In 1964 Eduardo Frei, a Christian Democrat, defeated Salvador Allende, the candidate of the popular front *(Frente de Acción Popular),* which was essentially a coalition of the Chilean Communist and Socialist parties. Frei's campaign was financially supported by the United States.
8. José Tohá, minister of the interior and later minister of defense under Allende, died while jailed in a military hospital in March 1974. Jorge Timossi, an Argentine journalist, covered Chile for the Prensa Latina agency from 1970 to 1973.
9. The War of the Triple Alliance (1865–1870) was fought by Paraguay against Brazil, Argentina, and Uruguay and resulted in the death of the vast majority of Paraguayan men.
10. Vladimir Herzog, a journalist, was news director of *TV Cultura,* an official organ of the state of São Paulo.
11. Carpentier, one of Cuba's most famous novelists and writers, died in April 1980.
12. Juan Rulfo has written only one novel, yet he is one of Mexico's leading novelists.
13. This is a reference to José Artigas, who led the fight for freedom in Uruguay from 1811 to 1820. He proposed the expropriation of property of foreigners and large landowners be parceled into small nontransferable plots given to the peasants.
14. Haroldo Conti was an Argentine novelist, professor, and filmmaker; he was kidnapped and officially disappeared.
15. Héctor Tizón is an Argentine novelist and short story writer.
16. All of these mechanical terms also refer to forms of torture: submarine to repeated and prolonged dunking, sawhorse to being forced to sit astride a sawhorse with a sharp blade on the top.
17. Bola de Nieve was a famous black Cuban singer who died in 1971.
18. This is a pun on the words *pescado* (fish) and *pecado* (sin).
19. Turquino is the highest mountain in Cuba.

IN DEFENSE OF THE WORD

Leaving Buenos Aires, June 1976

– 1 –

One writes out of a need to communicate and to commune with others, to denounce that which gives pain and to share that which gives happiness. One writes against one's solitude and against the solitude of others. One assumes that literature transmits knowledge and affects the behavior and language of those who read, thus helping us to know ourselves better and to save ourselves collectively. But "others" is too vague; and in times of crisis, times of definition, ambiguities may too closely resemble lies. One writes, in reality, for the people whose luck or misfortune one identifies with-the hungry, the sleepless, the rebels, and the wretched of this earth—and the majority of them are illiterate. Among the literate minority, how many can afford to buy books? Is this contradiction resolved by proclaiming that one writes for that facile abstraction known as "the masses"?

– 2 –

We were not born on the moon, we don't live in seventh heaven. We have the good fortune and the misfortune to belong to a tormented region of the world, Latin America, and to live in a historic period that is relentlessly oppressive. The contradictions of class society are sharper here than in the rich countries. Massive misery is the price paid by the poor countries so that 6 percent of the world's population may consume with impunity half the wealth generated by the entire world. The abyss, the distance between the well-being of some and the misery of others, is greater in Latin America; and the methods necessary to maintain this distance are more savage.

The development of a restrictive and dependent industry, which was superimposed on the old agrarian and mining structures without changing the latter's essential distortions, has sharpened social contradictions rather than alleviating them. The skills of the traditional politicians—experts in the arts of seduction and swindling—are today inadequate, antiquated, useless. The populist game which granted concessions—the better to manipulate—is no longer possible in some cases, and in others it reveals its dangerous double edge. Thus the dominant classes and countries resort to their repressive apparatuses. How else could a social system survive which more and more resembles a concentration camp? How, without barbed-wire fences, keep within bounds the growing legion of the damned? To the extent that the system finds itself threatened by the relentless growth of unemployment, poverty, and the resultant social and political tensions, room for pretense and good manners shrinks: in the outskirts of the world the system reveals its true face.

Why not recognize a certain sincerity in the dictatorships that today oppress the majority of our countries? Freedom of enterprise means, in times of crisis, the deprivation of freedom for people. Latin American scientists emigrate, laboratories and universities have no funds, industrial "know-how" is always foreign and exorbitantly expensive; but why not recognize a certain creativity in the development of a technology of terror? Latin America is making inspired universal contributions to the development of methods of torture, techniques for assassinating people and ideas, for the cultivation of silence, the extension of impotence, and the sowing of fear.

How can those of us who want to work for a literature that helps to make audible the voice of the voiceless function in the context of this reality? Can we make ourselves heard in the midst of a deaf-mute culture? The small freedom conceded to writers, is it not at times a proof of our failure? How far can we go? Whom can we reach?

A noble task, that of heralding the world of the just and the free; a noble function, that of rejecting a system of hunger and of cages—visible and invisible. But how many yards to the border? How long will those in power continue to give us their permission?

— 3 —

There has been much discussion of direct forms of censorship imposed by diverse sociopolitical regimes, of the prohibition of books or newspapers that are embarrassing or dangerous to them, and the exile, imprisonment, or murder of writers and journalists. But indirect censorship functions more subtly; it is no less real for being less apparent. Little is said about it, yet it is what most profoundly defines the oppressive and excluding character of the system to which most Latin American countries are subjected. What is the nature of this censorship which does not declare itself? It resides in the fact that the boat does not sail because there is no water in the sea; if only 5 percent of the Latin American population can buy refrigerators, what percentage can buy books? And what percentage can read them, feel a need for them, absorb their influence?

Latin American writers, wage workers in a cultural industry which serves the consumption needs of an enlightened elite, come from, and write for, a minority. This is the objective situation of both those writers whose work condones social inequity and the dominant ideology and those who attempt to break with it. We are, to a large extent, blocked by the game rules of the reality in which we function.

The prevailing social order perverts or annihilates the creative capacity of the immense majority of people and reduces the possibility of creation—an age-old response to human anguish and the certainty of death—to its professional exercise by a handful of specialists. How many "specialists" are we in Latin America? For whom do we write, whom do we reach? Where is our real public? (Let us mistrust applause. At times we are congratulated by those who consider us innocuous.)

– 4 –

One writes in order to deflect death and strangle the specters that haunt us; but what one writes can be historically useful only when in some way it coincides with the need of the collectivity to achieve its identity. This, I think, is what one wants. In saying: "This is who I am," in revealing oneself, the writer can help others to become aware of who they are. As a means of revealing collective identity, art should be considered an article of prime necessity, not a luxury. But in Latin America access to the products of art and culture is forbidden to the immense majority.

For the peoples whose identity has been shattered by the successive cultures of conquest, and whose merciless exploitation contributes to the functioning of the machinery of world capitalism, the system generates a "mass culture." Culture for the masses is a more precise description of this degraded art of the mass media, which manipulates consciousness, conceals reality, and stifles the creative imagination. Naturally it does not lead to a revelation of identity but is rather a means of erasing or distorting it in order to impose ways of life and patterns of consumption which are widely disseminated through the mass media. The culture of the dominant class is called "national culture"; it lives an imported life and limits itself to imitating, stupidly and vulgarly, so-called universal culture—or that which passes for such among those who confuse it with the culture of the dominant countries. In our time, an era of multiple markets and multinational corporations, both economics and culture (that is, "mass culture") have been internationalized, thanks to accelerated development and the mass media. The centers of power export not only machinery and patents to us, but also ideology. If in Latin America the enjoyment of worldly goods is limited to the few, it then follows that the majority must resign itself to the consumption of fantasy. Illusions of wealth are sold to the poor, illusions of freedom to the oppressed, dreams of victory to the defeated and of power to the weak. One need not be literate to consume the inviting symbols presented by television, radio, and films in their effort to justify the unequal organization of the world.

In order to maintain the status quo in these lands, where each minute a child dies of disease or hunger, we must look at ourselves through the eyes of those who oppress us. People are trained to accept this order as natural, therefore eternal; and the system is identified with the fatherland, so that an enemy of the regime is by extension a traitor or a foreign agent. The law of the jungle, which is the law of the system, is sanctified, so that the defeated peoples will accept their condition as destiny; by falsifying the past, the true causes of Latin America's historical failure are passed over—Latin America, whose poverty has always fed alien wealth. On the small television screen and on the large, the best man wins, the best being the strongest. The waste, the exhibitionism, and the unscrupulousness produce not revulsion but admiration; everything can be bought, sold, rented, consumed, including the soul. Magical properties are attributed to a cigarette, a car, a bottle of whiskey, or a wristwatch: they can provide us with personalities, they can guide us toward success and happiness. The proliferation of foreign heroes and role models parallels the fetishism of brand names and fashions of the rich countries. The local *fotonovelas** and soap operas take place in a limbo of pretentiousness, peripheral to the real social

*A *fotonovela* is a story of the romance genre, presented in comic book form and illustrated with photographs in place of cartoons.

and political problems of each country; and the imported serials sell Western, Christian democracy together with violence and tomato sauce.

– 5 –

In these lands of young people—young people whose numbers grow incessantly and who find no employment—the tick-tock of the time bomb obliges those who rule to sleep with one eye open. The multiple methods of cultural alienation—mechanisms used to drug and to castrate—take on increasing importance. The formulas for the sterilization of consciousness are put into practice with greater success than those for birth control.

The best way to colonize consciousness is to suppress it. In this sense also, the importation, whether deliberate or not, of a false counterculture, which finds a growing echo in the rising generations of some Latin American countries, plays a role. Those countries which do not offer the option of political participation—because of the fossilization of their structures or because of their stifling mechanisms of repression—offer the most fertile ground for the proliferation of a so-called culture of protest, originating outside the country, a sub-product of the leisure and waste which is focused on all social classes and originates in the spurious anticonventionalism of the parasite classes.

The customs and symbols of the resurgent youth of the sixties in the United States and Europe, born of a reaction against the uniformity of consumption, have become objects of assembly-line production in Latin America. Clothing with psychedelic designs is sold, accompanied by exhortations to "free yourself"; music, posters, hair styles, and clothing that reproduce the esthetic models of drug hallucination become mass-market items for the third world. Together with the symbols, colorful and appealing as they are, tickets to limbo are offered to young people who are attempting to flee the inferno. The new generations are invited to abandon a history which is painful for a trip to Nirvana. By joining this "drug culture" certain young Latin Americans achieve the illusion of reproducing the lifestyle of their metropolitan counterparts.

Originating in the lack of conformity of marginal groups in industrial alienated society, this false counterculture has nothing to do with our real needs of identity and destiny; it provides adventures for the immobilized; it generates resignation, egotism, noncommunication; it leaves reality intact but changes its image; it promises painless love and warless peace. Furthermore, by converting sensations into consumer goods, it dovetails perfectly with the "supermarket ideology" disseminated by the mass media. If the fetishism of cars and refrigerators is not sufficient to mute anguish and to calm anxieties, it is at least possible to buy peace, intensity, and happiness in the underground supermarket.

– 6 –

To awaken consciousness, to reveal reality—can literature claim a better function in these times and in these lands of ours? The culture of the system, the culture of reality—substitutes, disguises reality and anesthetizes consciousness. But what can a writer do-however much his or her flame burns—against the ideological mechanisms of lies and conformism?

If society tends to organize itself in such a way that contact between humans is precluded, and human relations are reduced to a sinister game of competition and consumption—of isolated individuals using and abusing each other—what role can be played by a literature of fraternal ties and collective solidarity? We have reached a point where to name things is to denounce them: but, to whom and for whom?

– 7 –

Our own fate as Latin American writers is linked to the need for profound social transformations. To narrate is to give oneself: it seems obvious that literature, as an effort to communicate fully, will continue to be blocked from the start, so long as misery and illiteracy exist, and so long as the possessors of power continue to carry out with impunity their policy of collective imbecilization, through the instruments of the mass media.

I don't share the attitude of those who demand special freedom for writers, independently of freedom for other workers. Great changes, deep structural changes, will be necessary in our countries if we writers are to go beyond the citadels of the elites, if we are to express ourselves, free of visible and invisible restraints. In an incarcerated society, free literature can exist only as denunciation and hope.

At the same time, I think that it would be a midsummer night's dream to imagine that the creative potential of the people could be realized through cultural means alone—the people, who were lulled to sleep long ago by harsh conditions of existence and the exigencies of life. How many talents have been extinguished in Latin America before they could reveal themselves? How many writers and artists have never had the opportunity to recognize themselves as such?

— 8 —

Furthermore, can a national culture be achieved completely in countries where the material bases of power are not indigenous but are dependent on foreign metropoli?

This being the case, does it make sense to write? There is no "degree zero" of culture, just as there is no "degree zero" of history. If we recognize an inevitable continuity between the stage of domination and the stage of liberation in any process of social development, why negate the importance of literature and its possible revolutionary role in the exploration, revelation, and diffusion of our real and potential identity? The oppressor does not want the mirror to reflect anything to the oppressed but its quicksilver surface. What process of change can activate a people that doesn't know who it is, nor from whence it comes? If it doesn't know who it is, how can it know what it deserves to become? Cannot literature aid, directly or indirectly, in this revelation?

It seems to me that the possibility of contribution depends to a large extent on the level of intensity of the writer's responsiveness to his or her people—their roots, their vicissitudes, their destiny and the ability to perceive the heartbeat, the sound and rhythm, of the authentic counterculture, which is on the rise. That which is considered "uncultured" often contains the seeds or fruits of another culture, which confronts the dominant one and does not share its values or its rhetoric. It is frequently and erroneously dismissed as a mere degraded imitation of the "culture products" of the elite or of the cultural models turned out by the system on an assembly-line basis. But a popular narrative is oftentimes more revealing and more meaningful than a "professional" novel, and the pulse of life is conveyed more forcefully in certain anonymous folksong couplets than in many volumes of poetry written in the code of the initiated. The testimonies of the people as they express in a thousand ways their tribulations and their hopes are more eloquent and beautiful than the books written "in the name of the people."

Our authentic collective identity is born out of the past and is nourished by it—our feet tread where others trod before us; the steps we take were prefigured—but this identity is not frozen into nostalgia. We are not, to be sure, going to discover our hidden countenance in the artificial perpetuation of customs, clothing, and curios which tourists demand of conquered peoples. We are what we do, especially what we do to change what we are: our identity resides in action and in struggle. Therefore, the revelation of what we are implies the denunciation of those who stop us from being what we can become. In defining ourselves our point of departure is challenge, and struggle against obstacles.

A literature born in the process of crisis and change, and deeply immersed in the risks and events of its time, can indeed help to create the symbols of the new reality, and perhaps—if talent and courage are not lacking—throw light on the signs along the road. It is not futile to sing the pain and the beauty of having been born in America.

– 9 –

Neither press runs nor sales figures necessarily provide a valid measure of the impact of a book. At times the written work radiates an influence much greater than is apparent; at times, it answers—years in advance—the questions and needs of the collectivity, if the writer has known how to experience them first, through inner doubts and agonies. Writing springs from the wounded consciousness of the writer and is projected onto the world; the act of creation is an act of solidarity which does not always fulfill its destiny during the lifetime of its creator.

– 10 –

I do not share the attitude of those writers who claim for themselves divine privileges not granted to ordinary mortals, nor of those who beat their breasts and rend their clothes as they clamor for public pardon for having lived a life devoted to serving a useless vocation. Neither so godly, nor so contemptible. Awareness of our limitations does not imply impotence: literature, a form of action, is not invested with supernatural powers, but the writer may become something of a magician if he or she procures, through a literary work, the survival of significant experiences and individuals.

If what is written is read seriously and to some extent changes or nourishes the consciousness of the reader, a writer has justified his or her role in the process of change: with neither arrogance nor false humility, but with the recognition of being a small part of something vast.

It seems to me appropriate that those who reject the word are the ones who cultivate monologues with their own shadows and with their endless labyrinths; but the word has significance for those of us who wish to celebrate and share the certainty that the human condition is not a cesspool. We seek interlocutors, not admirers; we offer dialogue, not spectacle. Our writing is informed by a desire to make contact, so that readers may become involved with words that came to us from them, and that return to them as hope and prophecy.

– 11 –

To claim that literature on its own is going to change reality would be an act of madness or arrogance. It seems to me no less foolish to deny that it can aid in making this change. The awareness of our limitations is undoubtedly an awareness of our reality. Amidst the fog of desperation and doubt, it is possible to face it and wrestle with it—with our limitations, but at the same time in opposition to them.

In this respect a "revolutionary" literature written for the convinced is just as much an abandonment as is a conservative literature devoted to the ecstatic contemplation of one's own navel. There are those who cultivate an "ultra" literature of apocalyptic tone, addressed to a limited public, convinced beforehand of what it proposes and transmits. What risk do these writers run, however revolutionary they claim to be, if they write for the minority that thinks and feels as they do, and if they give that minority what it expects? In such cases there is no possibility of failure; neither is there a possibility of success. What is the use of writing, if not to challenge the blockade imposed by the system on the dissenting message?

Our effectiveness depends on our capacity to be audacious and astute, clear and appealing. I would hope that we can create a language more fearless and beautiful than that used by conformist writers to greet the twilight.

– 12 –

But it is not only a problem of language; it is also one of media. The culture of resistance employs all the means available to it, and does not grant itself the luxury of wasting any vehicle or opportunity of expression. Time is short, the challenge a burning one, the task enormous; for a Latin American writer, enlisted in the cause of social change, the production of books constitutes one sector on a front of multiple efforts. We do not share the sanctification of literature as a frozen institution of bourgeois culture. Mass-market narrative and reportage, television, film, and radio scripts, popular songs are not always minor "genres" of inferior character, as is claimed by certain lords of specialized literary discourse, who look down on them. The fissures opened by Latin American rebel journalism in the alienating mechanisms of the mass media have frequently been the result of dedicated and creative works, which need no apology for their esthetic level or their efficacy when compared with good novels and short stories.

– 13 –

I believe in my vocation; I believe in my instrument. I cannot understand why those writers write who declare airily that writing makes no sense in a world where people are dying of hunger. Nor can I understand those who convert the word into the target of their rage and into a fetish. Words are weapons, and they can be used for good or for evil; the crime can never be blamed on the knife.

I think that a primordial function of Latin American literature today is the rescue of the word, frequently used and abused with impunity for the purpose of hampering and betraying communication.

"Freedom" in my country is the name of a jail for political prisoners, and "democracy" forms part of the title of various regimes of terror; the word "love" defines the relationship of a man with his automobile, and "revolution" is understood to describe what a new detergent can do in your kitchen; "glory" is something that a certain smooth soap produces in its user, and "happiness" is a sensation experienced while eating hot dogs. "A peaceful country" means, in many countries of Latin America, "a well-kept cemetery," and sometimes "healthy man" must be read as "impotent man."

By writing it is possible to offer, in spite of persecution and censorship, the testimony of our time and our people—for now and for later. One may write as if to say: "We are here, we were here; we are thus, we were thus." In Latin America a literature is taking shape and acquiring strength, a literature that does not lull its readers to sleep, but rather awakens them; that does not propose to bury our dead, but to immortalize them; that refuses to stir the ashes but rather attempts to light the fire. This literature perpetuates and enriches a powerful tradition of combative words. If, as we believe, hope is preferable to nostalgia, perhaps that nascent literature may come to deserve the beauty of the social forces which, sooner or later, by hook or by crook, will radically alter the course of our history. And perhaps it may help to preserve for the generations to come—in the words of the poet—"the true name of all things."